ONE CRAZY SUMMER . . .

Goals for the Week of June 9–15

1) *Read one book at age-appropriate reading level.*

2) *Do 10 pages in the Sixth-Grade Math Review Workbook.*

3) *Limit TV to two hours a day—educational programs only.*

4) *Survive the first week of Intensive Summer Language Learning.*

5) *Survive the first week of babysitting for Edison Blue.*

6) *Try not to think about what the other guys are doing at the pool.*

7) *Try not to think about what the other guys are doing at the park.*

8) *Remember that summer is only 10 weeks long. Motto: This too shall pass.*

CLAUDIA MILLS

You're a Brave Man, Julius Zimmerman

SCHOLASTIC INC.

New York Toronto London Auckland Sydney
Mexico City New Delhi Hong Kong Buenos Aires

ISBN 0-439-30936-0

12 11 10 9 8 7 6 5 4 3 2 1   1 2 3 4 5 6/0

Printed in the U.S.A.   40

First Scholastic printing, September 2001

To Beverly Reingold,
again and always,
and this time to Abby Sider, too

You're a Brave Man,
Julius Zimmerman

1

At nine o'clock in the morning on the first day of summer vacation, when he should have been sleeping late or heading off to the pool, Julius Zimmerman was speaking French. Not really *speaking* French, but he was opening his mouth, and French words, words in the French language, were coming out.

"*Bonjour, Madame Cowper,*" Julius repeated with all the others. "*Comment allez-vous?*" He knew he was saying it all wrong. When it came to school, even to summer school, Julius usually did everything all wrong.

"*Non! Non! Non!*" Madame Cowper, whose real

name was Mrs. Cowper, corrected them emphatically. Julius had already learned that the word for "No" in French is *"Non,"* pronounced with a long "o" to rhyme with *bone*, but said in a funny, nasal way, as if the speaker had a terrible, stuffy head cold and didn't know enough to blow his nose.

"Non! Non! Non! Comme ça! Like this!" Madame Cowper paused and then repeated the phrase, drawing out each syllable with exaggerated enunciation. When she said "Cowper," it sounded like "Cow-pear," but with about five "r"s at the end: "Cow-pearrrrr." If a word had one "r" in it, why give it five? When she said *"vous,"* her lips pursed as if she were about to kiss somebody. Julius couldn't believe how much work it was in French to say, "Good morning, how are you?" He wished they would learn the French for "Goodbye, I'm outta here." And then all go home.

He caught the eye of his best friend, Ethan Winfield, and they shared a quick grimace. It was Julius's fault, not Ethan's, that they were going to be spending three hours a day, five days a week, for five whole weeks in Intensive Summer Language Learning. Or, rather, it was Julius's mother's fault. She had found out about the program first, and signed up Julius, and then she had told Ethan's mother about it, and Mrs. Winfield had signed up Ethan, too.

Other kids' mothers must have found out about it, as well, because there were twenty-three students in

4

the class, even some other boys, like Alex Ryan, who looked as sheepish as Julius felt. Only Lizzie Archer, AKA the Lizard, seemed to be in her element. Lizzie had a long-standing crush on Ethan and was probably looking forward to being able to write bilingual love poems to him, half in English, half in French.

When the class finally satisfied Madame Cowper on "How are you?" she turned to the chalkboard. From the front, she was a remarkably large woman; from the rear, she looked even larger.

Alex leaned forward. "Madame *Cow*per. Get it?"

Marcia Faitak giggled.

Julius hoped Madame Cowper hadn't heard. If she had, she didn't show it. She wrote on the board, in large, neat handwriting: *Je m'appelle* _____ .

Then she turned back to the class and adjusted her glasses. They were definitely strange-looking glasses, the tortoiseshell frames rising to a pointy little peak on the outside of each eye. Had she actually picked out those frames on purpose at the glasses store? Maybe they had been the only pair on sale.

"Je m'appelle Madame Cowper," Madame Cowper said then. *"Comment vous appelez-vous?"* She stood still, obviously waiting for someone to answer.

Julius didn't get it. How could you give an answer when you didn't understand the question? He looked at Ethan. Ethan plainly didn't get it, either.

"Je m'appelle Madame Cowper. Comment vous

5

appelez-vous?" Madame Cowper repeated, her voice registering a hint of impatience.

Lizzie Archer raised her hand. *"Je m'appelle Lizzie Archer,"* she ventured.

"Bien! Bien! Good! Good! *Elle s'appelle Lizzie Archer. Comment vous appelez-vous?"* Madame Cowper pointed at Ethan.

Ethan managed to give his answer: *"Je m'appelle Ethan Winfield."*

Julius had begun to figure out that they were supposed to say their names. Okay, he could do that. He could say his name. He had had plenty of practice over the past twelve years saying his name.

One by one, almost all of them got through their names, though Marcia started to giggle again during hers, and when Alex said his, it sounded a lot like *"Je MOO-pelle Alex Ryan. Comment MOO appelez-MOO?"* Madame Cowper pretended not to notice. So she must have heard Alex's remark before.

Julius felt himself getting more and more nervous as his turn approached. All he had to do was say one sentence in French. That couldn't be so hard—even if he was going to have to speak French all by himself this time, just him, saying those strange, unintelligible words.

Finally Madame Cowper pointed at Julius. *"Comment vous appelez-vous?"*

Julius swallowed hard. Maybe he didn't have to say

the whole sentence. She had asked for his name; well, he'd tell her his name. "Julius Zimmerman," he said.

"*Non! Non! Non!* You must say, '*Je m'appelle Julius Zimmerman.*' " Madame Cowper adjusted her glasses again as she waited for Julius to repeat the full sentence.

He had heard the sentence twenty times already. Why couldn't he remember it now?

"*Je m'appelle . . .*" Madame Cowper prompted him.

"*Je m'appelle,*" Julius repeated miserably.

"Your name, Monsieur Zimmerman. You must say your name."

"Julius. I mean, Julius Zimmerman."

"*Non, non.* You must say, '*Je m'appelle Julius Zimmerman.*' "

Somehow Julius stammered it out. He thought he heard Alex say, "*Je m'appelle Julius Ding-Dong.*"

Forty-five minutes into Intensive Summer Language Learning, it was already clear who was the worst student in the class. It felt strangely familiar. It felt strangely like the rest of Julius's life.

Julius could still hear his mother explaining her plans for his summer. "Listen, honey, last summer we had a lazy summer, and I admit it was a lot of fun, but then—well, lazy habits developed over the summer can be hard to break, and you have to be disappointed, too, about your report cards this past year. So this summer

7

we're going to concentrate on setting a good foundation for seventh grade."

A good foundation, Julius was finding out, meant Intensive Summer Language Learning in the morning, and a *job* in the afternoon, which he would be starting in another few hours. His mother had read that jobs helped adolescents learn about responsibility, so she had signed him up to babysit for one of the children from Ethan's mother's preschool. She had pointed out that this way he'd have spending money of his own, plus he could start his own savings account for college. *College!* And a good foundation meant keeping a weekly goal-setting journal. Julius's mother loved goals and resolutions. She was the only person Julius knew who, in addition to New Year's resolutions, made new month's and new week's resolutions, too.

"Now, I'm not going to be reading your journal," she had told Julius when she handed him the green-covered, seventy-page, college-ruled, spiral-bound notebook. "But I want you to promise that you'll write in it faithfully."

Julius had promised. It wasn't as if he had a choice. So that morning he had written on the first page:

Goals for the Week of June 9–15
1. *Read one book at age-appropriate reading level.*

2. *Do 10 pages in the Sixth-Grade Math Review Workbook.*
3. *Limit TV to two hours a day—educational programs only.*
4. *Survive the first week of Intensive Summer Language Learning.*
5. *Survive the first week of babysitting for Edison Blue.*
6. *Try not to think about what the other guys are doing at the pool.*
7. *Try not to think about what the other guys are doing at the park.*
8. *Remember that summer is only 10 weeks long. Motto: This too shall pass.*

It was a pretty grim list. His mother had suggested the first three items on it; she had signed him up for the next two. Only the last three were his own, plus the motto. So far he hadn't even survived the first hour of the first day of Intensive Summer Language Learning. He still had a lot of goals to go.

At last Madame Cowper announced that it was time for a fifteen-minute break. When they returned, they would watch a video on France and learn some French songs. Julius bet the songs would be *"Frère Jacques"* and *"Sur le Pont d'Avignon."* He hoped they wouldn't have to all hold hands and dance. The image of

Madame Cowper skipping back and forth on the bridge of Avignon made Julius grin to himself, but he stifled the thought. Tall and gangly, he had been the butt of enough klutz jokes to cure him permanently of wanting to laugh at how anybody else looked.

It felt good to be outside, however briefly. Julius and Ethan slumped down on the blacktop, their backs against the brick wall of West Creek Middle School, where all the summer language programs were being held. Alex ambled over to join them.

"So what do you think of the Cow?" Alex asked.

"She's okay," Julius said uncomfortably.

"Okay? You've got to be kidding. Like, is this for real? We're going to be doing this all summer?"

"Just five weeks," Ethan said. Right then it sounded to Julius like a very long time.

"Five *weeks*? Five weeks out of our *lives*?" Alex's voice rose to an indignant squawk.

"Do you have to take it?" Julius asked. "Like, would your parents let you drop it? My mom's making me take it." *And* making him work a job. *And* making him read age-appropriate books.

"Mine, too," Ethan said, though Julius knew that Ethan's mother would let him drop it if he wanted to. Julius also knew that Ethan was the kind of friend who would never desert him. They had been friends since second grade, through thick and thin.

"My dad's going to France on a business trip this

fall, and he's taking my mom and me," Alex said. "They want me to learn a little French before we go."

Well, Julius wasn't going to France. He wasn't going anywhere. Nowhere fast, that was where he was headed.

"What do you say we shoot some hoops?" Ethan asked. "I brought my ball."

They had just enough time for Julius to miss two baskets before Madame Cowper appeared at the door, saying something to them in French that apparently meant it was time for the video. Julius barely watched it, and he tuned out during *"Frère Jacques"* and *"Sur le Pont."* Then they spent the rest of the morning discussing the weather. Julius learned that *"Il fait beau"* meant "The weather is beautiful." It was, too: clear, sunny, hot, but not too hot, perfect weather for biking, swimming, basketball, hiking—anything but Intensive Summer Language Learning.

When Julius biked home for lunch, his mother was there to greet him. She worked at home most days. She was a writer, but she didn't write novels or short stories or poetry, although Julius knew she wanted to. She wrote computer manuals. Boring computer manuals. Every once in a while she tried to slip in a little humor, she had told Julius, but the editors always took it out.

"Hi, honey. How *was* it?"

It was an ordinary question, but the tone was too ea-

11

ger. Julius knew she wanted him to say that he had fallen in love with the French language and that at long last he had discovered the subject that would turn him into a straight-A student.

"It was okay."

Her face showed a flicker of disappointment. Disappointing his mother was the one thing that Julius *was* good at.

"What's your teacher like?"

Should he tell her? No. She had enough problems of her own, writing dry, dull manuals all day when she wanted to write Pulitzer Prize–winning novels.

"She was okay, too."

"What's her name?"

"Mrs. Cowper. Only we have to call her Madame Cow-pear."

"I take it she's not another Ms. Gunderson?"

Julius flushed. Ms. Gunderson was the beautiful student science teacher who had come to West Creek Middle School last winter. Half the boys had had crushes on her, including Julius and Ethan. She had liked Ethan best, probably because Ethan had knocked himself out to impress her with a super-duper science fair experiment. For a while there, Julius had been pretty annoyed with Ethan. But now Ms. Gunderson was a fond memory, Julius was best friends with Ethan again, and Julius was through with love forever.

"No," he said. "She's not another Ms. Gunderson."
It was the understatement of the millennium.

"Oh, you're going to be so glad you took this course. Think how far ahead you'll be when you start a foreign language in eighth grade," his mother said.

Did she really believe that? She wouldn't if she had been in French class that morning, when Julius had been the only student in the room who couldn't even say his name. The question for Julius was never how far ahead he would be but how far behind. It was only the first day of Intensive Summer Language Learning, and already he felt so far behind that there was no way he could ever catch up.

2

As they ate their lunch of macaroni and tuna salad, Julius's mother kept using her hopeful-sounding, overly enthusiastic tone of voice. "And this afternoon you start your first *job*! Mrs. Blue told me on the phone that she knows you're going to be wonderful with little Edison. She thinks he'll do better with a male babysitter."

The comment suggested that Edison hadn't done particularly well with his last, female babysitter.

"And you'll be able to do all those fun *boy* things with him."

As if Julius weren't a total klutz at most "boy things."

"I'll try," he said lamely.

Apparently it was the right response. His mother's face brightened. "I know you will, honey. That's what it's all about in life: trying. Doing your best, whatever else happens."

Julius had met Edison and his parents briefly at his job interview two weeks ago. Edison had been pretty quiet and mopey from his nap, dragging a dingy blanket along behind him. Edison was three. In the mornings, he went to the Little Wonders preschool, where Ethan's mother was his teacher; in the afternoons, his mom stayed home with him. But this summer Mrs. Blue needed to work some extra hours and had decided to hire a babysitter to fill the gap. Mrs. Blue had called Mrs. Winfield, and Mrs. Winfield had called Mrs. Zimmerman. And the rest was history, as Custer had no doubt remarked when he looked up and saw the Indians.

At one o'clock on the dot, Julius rang the bell at the Blues' small brick split-level, about a mile's bike ride from home.

Mrs. Blue opened the door right away. She was short, considerably shorter than Julius. Her hair was pulled back in an untidy ponytail. "Oh, Julius, I'm so glad to see you. Come on in! Edison has been very . . ." She lowered her voice. "He thinks he doesn't want a babysitter. I'm afraid he's quite *adamant* about it. But

I'm sure you'll be able to win him over." Julius had never heard anybody sound less sure of anything.

"Edison!" Mrs. Blue called in the same falsely cheerful tone Julius had heard his own mother use an hour ago. Did all moms go to some special intensive summer course on gushing? Didn't they know kids figured out right away that the more cheerful their mothers sounded, the worse the fate that lay in store for them?

A small boy appeared in the doorway. He was wearing shorts and a T-shirt that said: "I ♡ Virginia Beach." But from the scowl that darkened his grubby little face, it looked as if Edison didn't ♡ anything.

"I don't think there's anything else I need to tell you before I go," Mrs. Blue said uncertainly. "Eat anything you want in the fridge. Be sure to put sunblock on Edison if you go out in the yard. I'm a little low on wipes, so use them sparingly. I'll be back at four. I've left his dad's and my work numbers on the bulletin board, in case there're any emergencies."

The mention of "emergencies" made Mrs. Blue look more uncertain than ever. She lowered her voice. "I've read that it's better for the mother not to prolong the goodbyes. The book said that even if the child cries, it's usually only for a minute or so, and it's worse if the mother lingers. But you'll tell me if he cries longer than that, won't you?"

Julius nodded numbly. He hoped Edison wouldn't cry. He hated it when people cried.

"Bye, angel!" His mother blew an obviously guilty kiss to Edison, who promptly burst into stormy sobs. Then she was gone. Julius's first afternoon of babysitting had begun.

Edison hurled himself at the front door, through which his mother had disappeared, beating his small fists against it.

"Hey, buddy," Julius said awkwardly. "She's coming back."

In three more hours.

Edison stood on his tiptoes and tried to turn the doorknob. To Julius's horror, the door began to open.

"Whoa!" Julius leaped forward to push it shut.

For the next few minutes, Edison strained to pull the door open, while Julius leaned against it to keep it closed. At least Julius had size and strength on his side. But Edison had willpower on his.

Something Mrs. Blue had said in parting was beginning to occupy the part of Julius's mind not taken up by his struggle with Edison. *Put sunblock on him.* That sounded bad enough: was Julius supposed to hold the door with one hand while he applied sunblock with the other? *Use wipes sparingly.* What kind of wipes? Did Edison howl so much that his parents bought special wipes for his chapped little nose? Or did she mean . . .

Julius looked down at Edison, still pulling at the door with all his might. Maybe his shorts did seem a little bulgy.

But the kid was three! He was a toddler, not a baby! Toddlers didn't wear diapers anymore—did they?

No. Julius's mother wouldn't have done this to him. She wouldn't have signed him up for a job where he would have to change diapers. He had never changed a diaper. He was never going to change a diaper. He didn't know how to change a diaper. Diapers had . . . *stuff* in them. Stuff Julius didn't even want to *think* about, let alone *look* at, let alone *wipe*.

"Come on, buddy," Julius said. "This is getting boring. Let's go do—" What? What did three-year-olds like to do? Besides have tantrums.

"I have an idea!" Julius said in an excited voice, as if he had reached into his pocket and found two free tickets to Disney World. "Why don't you show me your room? I bet you have a *cool* room!" Ten minutes into the job, Julius was already starting to sound like somebody's mother.

"No!" Edison said. But at least he let go of the doorknob. Julius grabbed the spare house key from the hook next to the door and quickly locked the deadbolt.

"Why don't you show me your toys?"

"No!"

"Why don't you show me your backyard?"

"No!"

Julius had an inspiration. "Why don't you show me nothing?"

"No!"

"You don't want to show me nothing? Okay, don't show me nothing. Show me something. What do you want to show me?""

Edison had to think that one over. "Nothing," he finally said, but Julius could tell Edison knew he had lost the first round.

"Ooh, I like your nothing!" Julius said. "Wow, Edison, that nothing is so cool!"

Edison giggled. Julius felt a small stir of satisfaction. So far, on the first day of summer, he had accomplished one thing. He hadn't been able to say his name in French, but he had made Edison Blue laugh.

Edison was still in a good mood when he finally led Julius upstairs to his room. "Edison's bed!" he shouted, leaping into the middle of a smaller-than-regular-size bed covered with a Winnie-the-Pooh bedspread.

He ran to the bureau. "Edison's clothes!"

He ran to what was unmistakably a changing table. A *diaper*-changing table.

"Edison's *diapers*!" The word caused him to burst into gales of laughter. Sure enough, there was a stack of disposable diapers in one of the bins beneath the changing table.

Julius's blood ran cold.

There was no way that he, Julius Zimmerman, was

going to change anybody's diaper. That was final. Edison was going to have to wait until four o'clock on weekday afternoons to put anything in his diapers. If he did pee or poop before then, Julius was going to pretend that it had happened as Mrs. Blue was walking in the door. Three hours wasn't that long. A kid could wait three little hours to have his diaper changed. Pioneer kids crossing the prairie in covered wagons had probably waited a lot longer than that.

Still, Julius wanted to get as far away from the changing table as possible. "Hey, buddy, show me Edison's yard."

He managed to get sunblock smeared on Edison's chubby arms and legs. His face was harder. Or rather, his face was impossible. On little kids' faces, everything was so close together that their cheeks and noses were right next to their eyes. Sunblock in your eyes could really sting. And the harder someone pulled away from you, the harder it was even to dab on sunblock, let alone rub it in. Julius got one little dot of sunblock on Edison's left cheek before he gave up, hoping that you couldn't get skin cancer in an afternoon.

Finally, they were ready to go outside. But as soon as they reached the large, square sandbox that stood next to the redwood play set, Edison turned difficult again. Instead of digging sand, he began throwing it. Julius could tell that he wasn't throwing sand because he wanted to throw sand; he was throwing sand to see if Julius would stop him.

Julius said his line: "Hey, buddy, no throwing sand."

Edison threw another handful of sand, a bigger handful this time.

Julius had tried being his mother; now he'd try being his father. He put on a sterner voice: "I said, *no throwing sand*."

Edison threw his sand toward Julius.

Maybe with Edison you had to explain the reason for a rule. "Look, buddy, if you throw sand, it can get in somebody's eye. In Edison's eye. Edison no like sand in eye. Edison have to go to doctor. Doctor dig sand out of Edison's eye. Ooh, that hurts Edison's eye."

Edison held his next handful of sand. Was he considering this line of argument, or wondering if his babysitter had suddenly lost the power to speak coherent English? Then he threw it.

Julius was getting angry now. He knew he wasn't allowed to spank Edison, but he could give him a time-out. Mrs. Blue had discussed "guidelines for discipline" with him at the interview. She had told him he could place Edison in a time-out chair for a couple of minutes. She had also told him that the only problem with this was that Edison wouldn't stay in a time-out chair for even a couple of seconds.

"That does it, buddy! You're in time-out!"

Julius swooped down and gathered up a kicking, screaming Edison and set him down on the picnic bench.

"No!" Edison ran back to the sandbox.

Again, Julius carried him to the picnic bench.

Edison ran back to the sandbox.

Was Julius supposed to hold him in the time-out chair? He could, if he had to.

He carried Edison to the picnic bench once more. This time he held Edison, squirming and struggling, in place. Julius might be a spindly version of a twelve-year-old, but compared to a three-year-old's, his physique was magnificent. He had Edison this time.

Until Edison bit him. On the hand. Hard.

"Owwww! You little—"

Edison burst free and ran back to the sandbox, to the exact same spot where he had been standing before Julius first carried him away.

Julius heard merry laughter. He looked up. Watching them from over the neighbors' fence was a girl. Apparently she had been watching the whole time.

3

If babysitting for Edison Blue was bad, worse was babysitting for Edison Blue in front of an audience.

"I suppose you could do better," Julius said defensively.

"I wouldn't even try," the girl said.

Julius remembered Mrs. Blue's remark to his mother about how Edison might do better with a male babysitter. He had a sneaking suspicion that this girl with the mocking eyes had been the female babysitter who hadn't worked out. It was only reasonable that the Blues would have started with their next-door neighbor before turning to him.

"I bet you did," he said. "I bet the only reason I'm here making a fool of myself is that you already tried and failed."

"You lose. I don't sign up to do things I'm going to fail at."

With the fence between them, Julius could see only her head and shoulders. She was around his height, and even though she looked sixteen, somehow Julius could tell that she only *looked* sixteen; he would guess that she was actually close to his own age. She was undeniably pretty, with straight dark hair that fell past her shoulders and large dark eyes. She certainly didn't look like someone who'd ever failed at anything.

Julius turned to check on Edison, who was still standing in the sandbox, silently watching them and *not* throwing sand. Julius realized that he had discovered something important: three-year-olds can be distracted.

He turned back to the girl again, wondering if he could steer the discussion in a friendlier direction. He wasn't used to chatting casually with someone who was so pretty.

"So do you babysit for any other kids?" Most of the girls Julius knew loved little kids and had counted the months until they were old enough to babysit.

The girl gave him a scornful look. "Life is too short."

She had a point there. Forget life: *summer* was too

short to spend babysitting, much less learning French, and yet somehow Julius was doing both.

Julius tried to think of something else to ask her. He wanted to prolong the conversation that was distracting Edison so effectively. "What do you do instead?"

"I dance. I sing. I act."

It was easy to imagine her on the stage. She was definitely a dramatic figure, with her dark coloring and her expressive face.

"Do you want to be an actress?" Julius asked.

"I *am* an actress. I played Juliet last year in the Waverly School's production of *Romeo and Juliet*." The Waverly School was a fancy private school. It figured. "And I'm auditioning for the Summertime Players production of *Oklahoma!* in a couple of weeks."

She studied Julius with what seemed to be genuine interest. "What about you? What do you do when you're not babysitting *l'enfant terrible*?"

Julius didn't understand the last part of the question, though something about it sounded vaguely familiar. *Lon-fon terrr-eebl*?

"It's French for 'the terrible child.' "

"Actually, I've been studying French." Maybe that would impress her.

"How long?" she demanded skeptically, as if anyone who had studied French for more than one day would know the French words for "terrible child."

"One day," Julius admitted. So much for impressing her.

"*Comment vous appelez-vous?*" she asked.

Wait a minute. He knew what *that* meant. Julius couldn't believe that less than two hours out of his first French class he was being asked a question in French that he could not only understand but maybe even answer. He gave it a try: "*Je m'appelle Julius Zimmerman.*"

He must have said it right, because the girl smiled. She had an incredible smile that seemed to say the person she was smiling at was her favorite person in the whole entire world. "*Je m'appelle Octavia Aldridge.*"

Julius glanced back to check on Edison again. A stinging handful of sand struck him on his bare arm.

"I think this is my cue for an exit," Octavia said. "*Au revoir, Julius.* I wish you luck. Lots of luck."

Julius didn't know if he was relieved or sorry to see her go. He glanced at his watch. Two more hours. Two more hours to be the target of Edison's sand-throwing.

Distraction, he remembered. Distraction was the key.

Julius suggested a nap. Edison didn't want to take a nap.

Julius suggested a story. Edison didn't want to hear a story.

Julius suggested a nap again. Kids small enough to be wearing diapers should still be taking afternoon naps. But Edison hadn't changed his anti-nap stance since the previous suggestion.

Then Julius suggested a snack. He himself was ravenous, as if he'd been working all day at hard labor on a chain gang. This time, Edison followed Julius into the kitchen.

The snack worked out pretty well, although Edison spilled his juice all over his I ♡ Virginia Beach shirt and had a tantrum when Julius wouldn't let him eat a crumbled cookie that had fallen onto the Blues' none-too-clean kitchen floor. In the end, Julius let him eat it. Kids had probably eaten worse things than that and survived.

It was only two-fifteen. Suddenly Julius remembered: TV. Edison's mother had told him at the job interview that she didn't want him and Edison to spend their time together staring at the TV, but Julius decided she couldn't possibly have meant it. Besides, they weren't spending their *whole* time together watching TV. Edison had spent almost half of it having tantrums.

Anyway, he'd turn it off at three fifty-five and hope that Edison had the sense not to tell.

Julius clicked around the channels until he found the Flintstones. He had written in his goals journal that he would watch two hours a day of TV, maximum, educational programs only, but surely cartoons with Edison didn't count toward his own limit.

Peace descended on the Blue household. There were

two couches in the family room. Julius sprawled on one. Edison sprawled on the other. The Flintstones were followed by Bugs Bunny. Bugs Bunny was followed by Porky Pig. The afternoon wasn't turning out so badly, after all.

At three-fifty, to be on the safe side, Julius announced in his now-perfected fake-cheerful voice, "All right, buddy! We have to let the TV rest now!"

No sooner had he clicked the power button than a loud wail arose from Edison.

"More TV!"

"No, no, buddy. The TV's tired. Poor TV! It needs to go for a nice little nap."

"TVs don't take naps!"

All right, so the kid wasn't dumb. "Well, it doesn't need to take a nap, exactly, but it can break if we don't turn it off for a while and let the circuits cool down."

Edison considered this explanation. He seemed to know that it was better than the first one Julius had given, but it still wasn't good enough.

"More TV!"

Julius was getting desperate. Desperate enough to try the truth. "Look, your mom said we weren't supposed to watch TV. She's going to be here any minute, and if she finds us watching TV, we're going to be in big trouble. Both of us. You and me."

The mention of Edison's mother turned out to be a mistake.

"I want my mommy!" The cry was so loud that Octavia could probably hear it a house away.

"She's coming! Any minute now!" At least Julius hoped she was. If she was late, he didn't know what he'd do.

But she wasn't late. Mrs. Blue appeared promptly at four, just as Edison had stopped shrieking, "I want my mommy!" and had gone back to shrieking, "More TV!"

Mrs. Blue flew to Edison and caught him up in a big hug. It wasn't a fake hug, either, as far as Julius could tell. Hard as it might be to believe, Edison's mother actually loved him.

Then, when Edison was finally quiet, Mrs. Blue turned to Julius. "How did it go?"

"Pretty well," Julius said, relieved that she hadn't asked what Edison had meant by crying "More TV!" And it *had* gone pretty well, all things considered. Edison hadn't pooped in his diaper, though Julius could smell that he had deposited a generous quantity of pee-pee in it. There had been no visit to the emergency room, no frantic calls to 911. The house was still standing.

"Julius, what was Edison saying about more TV?"

Julius kept his tone professional and polite. "I had some trouble getting him calmed down after his snack, so we watched a little bit toward the end."

"Just a little bit, though." Luckily she didn't pause for confirmation. "I guess that's all right. I know the

29

afternoons can get a bit . . . long sometimes. Speaking of which: angel, it's time for us to say goodbye to Julius."

"Bye, Edison!" Julius said. If there was ever a contest for the two most beautiful words in the English language, he had his entry ready.

"No! Julius stay!"

To Julius's great surprise, Edison sprang across the room and attached himself to Julius's leg.

"Hey, buddy, I'll be back! I promise!"

For the next few minutes, Julius's leg was the scene of a tug of war. Edison tugged on Julius's leg; Mrs. Blue tugged on Edison. Finally, fortunately for Julius, Mrs. Blue won.

Julius didn't linger for another round of farewells. He bolted out the door to freedom. Though he had to admit that he had found Edison's last tantrum oddly gratifying. Maybe you weren't a total failure as a babysitter if the kid cried when it was time for you to leave.

As he unlocked his bike, he heard from the family room the unmistakable theme music of Looney Tunes. Afternoons with Edison could get long, all right.

Julius made a beeline for Ethan's house. He and Ethan hung out and shot a few baskets until six o'clock. They were both lousy players, but liked playing, anyway. Then Julius headed home. His mom had a deadline looming on a writing project, and his dad was working late at his accounting office, so dinner was leftover Chinese carryout that Julius heated up for his mom and himself in the microwave.

"Okay, *now* tell me," his mom said as she picked up her chopsticks. "How was your first day at your very first *job*?" She emphasized the word as if Julius were a little kid, Edison's age, and she was trying to make him feel important. "Did you get off to a good start with Edison?"

Had he gotten off to a good start with Edison? His hand still hurt from where Edison had bit him, but he also still felt secretly pleased that Edison had cried when it was time for him to go. "I guess so," he said.

"What kinds of things did you do with him?"

Julius thought over his possible answers: *Let him bite me, let him throw sand at me, watched a bunch of dumb cartoons on TV.*

"Just things," he said.

His mother didn't look satisfied, but she changed the subject.

"I took a little break this afternoon and went to the library," she said. "I came home with more books than I can possibly read in two months, let alone two weeks, but I couldn't resist. How about you? Have you picked out which book you want to read this week?"

She had to be joking. It was only *Monday*. He wasn't going to start on his week's reading goal on a *Monday*. Besides, how could he come home from a morning

31

spent with Madame Cowper and an afternoon spent with Edison Blue and then spend his evening reading age-appropriate books and filling in pages in his Sixth-Grade Math Review Workbook? His mother couldn't expect him to attempt the impossible. Fortunately, he had made this discovery in time to revise his week's goals.

After dinner, Julius opened his green-covered journal and wrote:

> *Goals for the Week of June 9–15, Revised*
> 1. *Try not to make a fool of yourself in French class.*
> 2. *Get Edison Blue to stop throwing sand.*
> 3. *Limit Edison's TV to one hour per afternoon—no sex or violence.*
> 4. *Try to keep Edison from pooping in his diaper.*

It was a good thing his mother had said she wouldn't be reading his goals journal. Maybe he could reinstate the reading goal and the math goal when he had the summer more under control. *If* he ever had the summer more under control.

He studied the list again. Then he added:

> 5. *Find out more about Octavia Aldridge.*

4

After three more days of Intensive Summer Language Learning, Julius was an old pro at "My name is Julius Zimmerman" and "Good morning, how are you?" He was getting pretty good at "What is the weather like?" "It is fine." "It is raining." "It is snowing."

But he still felt it was a mistake on Madame Cowper's part to insist on talking to the class so much of the time in French. Hadn't she noticed that none of them could understand French? Unless the others all understood. Was Julius the only one who sat there in a fog of stupefaction?

And in less than five weeks they were going to have

to put on a play for their families and friends—performed entirely in French! That was what Madame Cowper had said—unless Julius had misunderstood her. Which was all too possible. She couldn't really have meant that he, Julius Zimmerman, was going to speak in French in front of an audience. Maybe it would be a play in which the characters mainly exchanged their names and talked about the weather.

At least they were also going to cook French foods. And eat French foods. Friday was to be their cooking day, and so on that Friday they met for class in the middle-school Family Living room.

Right away Madame Cowper said something in French that ended with the words *quiche Lorraine*. Julius decided she must be saying, "Today we will make quiche Lorraine." He had never heard of quiche Lorraine, but he figured it had to be a kind of food, and any kind of food sounded good to Julius.

He made sure to stick close to Ethan as they divided into groups of four for the cooking, each group claiming its own individual kitchenette, complete with stove, sink, and refrigerator. Unlike most of the kids Julius knew, and unlike Julius himself, Ethan could cook. Ethan and his older brother, Peter, cooked dinner at their house most Saturday nights. At Julius's house, nobody cooked on most nights. Julius's mother liked the joke, "What does a working mother make for dinner?" "Reservations!" In her case, it was phone calls for carryout pizza, carryout Chinese, carryout Vietnamese, and carryout Italian. There was no carryout French restaurant in the vicinity of West Creek, which was why the Zimmermans never ate quiche.

Alex and Marcia were in Julius's group, too. Lizzie was probably disappointed at not getting to be with Ethan, and Ethan was probably relieved at not having to be with Lizzie.

Madame Cowper held up a package of store-bought piecrusts. "Today we will cheat just a little bit," she said, speaking for once in plain ordinary English. "We will use packaged piecrusts for our quiche. But I must tell you that this the French would never do. *Non, jamais!* In France all the food is prepared fresh, from the freshest possible ingredients."

She demonstrated how to fit the piecrust into the piepan.

"I'll do ours," Marcia said importantly, snatching up their piecrust and awkwardly smooshing it in place. Julius was sure that Ethan was a better cook than Marcia.

"Look," Alex said in a loud whisper. "There's going to be one quiche for each group, and one for La Cow. A whole pie just for her." This time he oinked instead of mooing.

"*Maintenant, la préparation.* Now, the filling," Madame Cowper went on when all the piecrusts were in their pans and had been placed in the oven to bake for five minutes. "I must say this is going to be a very naughty day for dieters!"

"I bet it's not her first naughty day," Alex said.

Julius felt embarrassed for Madame Cowper. He wished she would explain the recipe without calling attention to how fattening it was. Didn't she know she was giving kids like Alex more opportunity for mean remarks?

"One of you can have my piece," Marcia said to the boys. "I'm trying to cut back on calories."

She looked at the others as if expecting one of them to say, "*You* don't need to worry about calories." And she didn't. Marcia was the skinniest girl in the class, except for Lizzie, who was the skinniest and the shortest.

"Yeah, you're really a tub," Alex said.

"I am not!" Marcia said, pretending to pout, but plainly pleased at how obviously false his statement was.

"Can you pinch an inch?" Alex leaned over to pinch whatever fat was available from Marcia's slim waist.

Julius was pretty sure that Alex liked Marcia. Marcia squealed and shoved him away. Maybe she liked him, too.

Madame Cowper gave them both a cold look. "Monsieur Ryan, Mademoiselle Faitak, I hope I will not have to ask anyone to leave during our first cooking demonstration."

Alex and Marcia stopped their horsing around, but they didn't look happy about it.

"As I was saying," Madame Cowper went on, "the filling for our quiche Lorraine is very rich. It is made of bacon, cheese, cream, and eggs. *Du bacon, du fromage, de la crème, des oeufs.* We will begin with the bacon."

Madame Cowper gave each group a slab of uncooked bacon to chop into one-inch pieces. Ethan efficiently chopped theirs and placed it in the frying pan, then set about capably separating the sizzling bacon pieces with a fork. Julius felt a quick surge of admiration for his friend, mingled with jealousy. Ethan liked to act as if he and Julius were lousy at all the same things—basketball, math—but Ethan was good at a lot of things, too. Having an older brother probably helped. When you were an only child, you had nobody to show you things. You fumbled and bumbled around on your own.

After Madame Cowper approved the doneness of their bacon, Ethan transferred the bacon bits onto a paper towel and then poured the fat from the pan into a waiting jar.

"Ick," Marcia said.

"That's what Madame Cow would look like if she melted. 'Help, I'm melting!' " Alex screeched in what was clearly intended to be an imitation of the Wicked Witch of the West.

"Monsieur Ryan," Madame Cowper called above the general din. "This is your second warning."

While Alex and Marcia prepared the egg and cream filling, Ethan set Julius to work dicing a block of Swiss cheese. Julius managed to do it without dicing any part of his fingers. Then, as directed by Madame Cowper, he scattered the cheese in the bottom of the piecrust, and Ethan sprinkled in the bacon bits.

"*Bien! Bien!* Now we will pour in our filling. *Comme ça!* Like this!" Madame Cowper demonstrated on her own quiche. It was true that she had made one just for herself.

Ethan poured in the filling, almost spilling it when Alex jostled him while trying to pinch another nonexistent inch of fat from Marcia's skinny frame.

"Monsieur Ryan! You have had two warnings. I do not give three warnings." Madame Cowper's voice was unpleasantly shrill. "I must ask you to leave us. You may sit in the hall outside our room and read in your textbook while the rest of us finish preparing our quiche. Needless to say, you will not be joining us when we eat our quiche, either."

At first Alex hesitated, as if he was thinking about defying Madame Cowper. But then he mustered a sneer and sauntered out to the hall.

"Now carefully, *very* carefully, carry your quiche to the oven. Place it on the center rack. It will need to bake for thirty-five to forty minutes."

Madame Cowper came over to their group. "Monsieur Zimmerman, will you do the honors?"

Julius swallowed hard. He had expected Ethan, the chef, or Marcia, the know-it-all girl, to do the honors. Madame Cowper apparently didn't know that his nickname in fifth grade had been Klutzius.

Ethan opened the oven door for him. The oven had been preheated, and Julius felt a blast of scorching-hot air.

Madame Cowper was still waiting. Julius picked up the quiche, his hands slightly shaking. The filling sloshed from one side of the pan to the other. It seemed alive.

"Be careful, Monsieur Zimmerman! *Faites attention!*"

If only she would stop watching him. Julius could never perform when people watched him. Having Madame Cowper watch him try to put a quiche in the oven was like having Octavia Aldridge watch him try to keep Edison Blue in time-out, or like having the whole class watch him try to stammer out his name. Some people performed better under pressure; Julius didn't.

Julius sensed the disaster before it happened. He

had a fleeting vision of losing control of the pan and spilling the quiche all over the floor. Then, just as he was about to slide it onto the rack, he lost control of the pan.

Julius watched, helpless, as the quiche spilled all over the oven door and dripped onto the floor.

Marcia giggled. Ethan groaned. Julius felt his cheeks flame hotter than the preheated oven.

Madame Cowper let his group eat her quiche. It made Julius feel better about Madame Cowper, but it didn't make him feel any better about himself.

That afternoon Julius took Edison in his stroller to the park, half a mile or so from the Blues' house. The stroller was one of the few things in his life that Edison definitely liked. All Julius had to do was strap him in, and off they went. When Julius was out pushing Edison in his stroller, he felt capable and purposeful, as if he knew what he was doing and where he was going. He felt the way Octavia Aldridge looked.

Compared to the quiche disaster, the past few days of babysitting for Edison Blue hadn't been too bad. Julius had avoided the backyard, in order to avoid the sandbox. This also meant that he had avoided Octavia, whom he hadn't particularly wanted to avoid. He felt the need to redeem himself somehow in her eyes. Of course, with Edison in tow, he could easily end up only embarrassing himself further.

At the park, Julius made the mistake of letting Edison out of his stroller to play, for within minutes Edison had figured out that the pleasures of throwing gravel were very like the pleasures of throwing sand.

"You're going to have to keep your little brother from throwing the gravel," one of the mothers there told him.

Did she really think Julius wanted his "little brother" to throw gravel? Did she really think Julius could stop his "little brother" from throwing gravel?

"Hey," Julius said to Edison. "Did you hear what the lady said? No throwing gravel."

Unimpressed, Edison continued to throw gravel.

"He could get that in somebody's eye," the woman said.

Julius tried again. "The lady doesn't like it when you do that."

More gravel flew by.

Julius had to do something. "Edison, if you don't stop, I'm putting you in your stroller right now and taking you home."

This time the flying gravel struck Julius's leg.

He had made the threat; now he had to carry it out. Wishing the lady weren't still watching him, he straightened his shoulders to signal that he meant business. But he had a hunch that forcing Edison into the stroller was not going to be particularly easy.

Sure enough, it wasn't.

Edison kicked and hit and bit. Somehow Julius succeeded at stuffing him in his seat and securing the seat belt. As the mothers watched, Julius wheeled the screaming Edison away from the park playground.

All the way home, Edison howled. Julius was surprised that nobody stopped them to accuse him of kidnapping. Not that anybody in his right mind would want to kidnap Edison Blue.

Octavia was in her front yard, sitting in a swing that hung from the big tree by the house. She was wearing a long white dress—her *Romeo and Juliet* costume, maybe. Her timing was impeccable.

"*Bonjour, Julius,*" she said. "I see Edison is his usual good-natured self today."

Julius felt better. Octavia had made it seem as if the problem lay with Edison's being Edison rather than with Julius's being Julius.

"He and I had a little disagreement over throwing gravel at the park," Julius said.

"And you won."

"If you call this winning." Julius wasn't sure he did. Edison's tears streaked the dirt that had mingled with the sunblock Julius had applied to his cheeks. At least Julius had learned how to get enough sunblock on his tiny face.

Octavia leaned back in the swing. "Do you mind if I ask you one question?"

"No," Julius said cautiously.

"Why?"

"Why what?"

"Why are you doing this?" She sounded as if she really wanted to know.

The question embarrassed him. "Why do you think? To earn money, that's why." Not that he had gotten any yet. Mrs. Blue was going to pay him every Friday, so he wouldn't get his first pay for another hour. He could hardly wait.

"No," Octavia said. "There're easier ways to earn money. I can think of at least five hundred."

Apparently, Julius hadn't fooled her. "My mom signed me up. She wants me to have a job this summer. I'm supposed to be learning about responsibility."

"And are you?"

Julius shrugged. He felt the color rising in his face. "I'm learning something, I guess."

Octavia laughed, not a mean laugh. "I bet you are."

Julius glanced down at Edison. He had fallen asleep. He seemed so innocent when he was sleeping. Octavia pushed off gracefully with her sandaled feet and resumed her swinging. Julius wheeled Edison around to the back of the house, then managed somehow to maneuver the stroller up the steps and inside the door. Whatever he was learning this summer, it was something he didn't particularly want to know.

5

Julius knew he was going to have to make some new goals for the coming week. He definitely didn't want the second week of summer vacation to be anything like the first. Reviewing the week's goals: he had made the biggest possible fool of himself in French class; he hadn't gotten Edison to stop throwing sand *or* gravel; he and Edison had watched more than an hour of TV on several days. He had had a conversation with Octavia, but instead of finding out more about her, he had let her find out more about him, which wasn't on his list at all. The only accomplishment he had to show for the week, when you got right down to it, was that Edison hadn't pooped in his diaper. That was it. Period.

Well, that wasn't quite all. He had earned the first non-allowance money of his life, and that felt pretty good. But what could he possibly buy with it that was worth what he had gone through to earn it?

His mother seemed worried about him, too, but for different reasons. "Honey, you didn't read *any* books this week?" she asked him on Sunday night, when he came home from playing water basketball with Ethan and some of the other guys at the pool. "I know you've been busy with your class and your job and your friends, but everyone needs to make time for *reading*."

Of course, she had been reading herself when he came in. She was always reading. Too bad he hadn't caught her at the end of the book. When his mother was within the last hundred pages of a book, the house could burn to the ground and she wouldn't notice. She usually cried at the end, too. Julius was invariably relieved when he saw that it was a book she was crying over, rather than the memory of his last report card.

Julius hesitated. "I started one, but I haven't finished it yet," he lied.

"What is it?" she asked eagerly.

"I—um—I don't remember the title."

She looked so disappointed that Julius tried to think of a title, any title. Ethan had read *A Tale of Two Cities* last year when he was trying to impress Ms. Gunderson.

"It was something about cities. Two cities. *A Tale of Two Cities*. That's it."

45

Her face brightened. "You're reading *A Tale of Two Cities*? Julius, that's a wonderful book! No wonder you didn't get it finished in a week. That's hardly a book you whip right through. And it fits in so perfectly with your French class, too."

Why did it fit in well with his French class? Were the two cities somewhere in France? Julius felt his face betraying him.

"You're not reading it." His mother turned away.

"But I'm *going* to," Julius said. He hated it when the light went out of her eyes that way, all because of him. "Ethan read it last year, and he said it was really good."

"I don't want you to read a book for me, I want you to read it for yourself."

"That's what I'm going to do. I'm going to read it for myself."

His father came in. Julius's dad was a tall, heavyset man, not a Mr. Cow, but someone who could stand to lose twenty pounds around his middle. Julius had seen pictures of his dad as a tall, skinny boy like himself. He sometimes wondered if he would have a middle like that someday, and wear a suit and carry a briefcase to his accounting office. The thought made his heart sink, although there wasn't anything else he was planning to become.

"You're going to read what for yourself?" his father asked.

46

"A Tale of Two Cities."

"Good luck," his father said.

"Dan! Don't discourage him! *A Tale of Two Cities* is a perfectly thrilling book. I loved it when I was his age."

His father gave Julius a look that said: I doubt you'll like it, but you might as well humor your mother. Come to think of it, his father didn't read books. He read two newspapers every morning, but Julius couldn't remember the last time he had seen his father reading a book.

Julius made a quick call to Ethan. "How long is *A Tale of Two Cities*?"

"Four hundred twenty-two pages." It didn't surprise Julius that Ethan could still give the exact answer. "Why?"

"My mom wants me to read it."

"It's good," Ethan said. "It starts out kind of slow, but then it gets good."

So Julius put it on his list.

Goals for the Week of June 16–22

1. *Make Ethan do all the cooking on cooking day.*

2. *Limit Edison to three tantrums a day, none in front of Octavia Aldridge.*

3. *Keep Edison from pooping in his diaper—* *VERY IMPORTANT!!!!*

4. Start reading A Tale of Two Cities, *by*
Charles Dickens (422 pages). Find out if the
cities are in France.

This week's list seemed even more gruesome than last week's. Week two of summer vacation looked as if it was going to be, if anything, worse than week one.

On Monday, Julius and Ethan passed Lizzie as they biked together to West Creek Middle School. She was walking. Julius had never seen Lizzie on a bike. Maybe she was the only kid in Colorado who couldn't ride one, just as last year she had been the only kid in Colorado who couldn't light a match to start the bunsen burner in science class.

Lizzie caught up with them while they waited at the next traffic light. "Hi," Julius said, to break the awkward silence.

"Hi," Ethan echoed.

Lizzie flushed with pleasure. Julius thought she'd probably sit all morning writing "Hi" over and over again in the notebook she always carried with her.

The light was taking a long time to change. Ethan was beginning to get the desperate, trapped look he often got around Lizzie. Julius tried to help out. "How's it going?" he asked her.

"Wonderful! Don't you love French? I dreamed I was

in Paris last night, living in a garret on the Left Bank, in the Latin Quarter, selling flowers on the streets all day and then writing poetry all night. By the light of one flickering candle."

"They have electricity in France," Julius couldn't resist pointing out.

"In my dream they didn't. Maybe it was long-ago Paris, like in *La Bohème*, or maybe I couldn't afford electricity because I was so poor and nobody would buy the flowers I was selling."

She paused. "Except you, Ethan. You were in my dream, too, and you were the only person who bought any flowers from me."

"The light's green now," Ethan said in a strangled voice.

"See you later," Julius said for both of them as they pushed off, Ethan in the lead, pedaling as furiously as a rider in the final time trial in the Tour de France.

Julius didn't usually tease Ethan about Lizzie— Ethan got teased enough by the other kids—but this time he couldn't help himself.

"What kind of flowers did you buy from her?" he asked when they were locking their bikes.

Ethan punched him in the arm. "Cut it out."

Lizzie arrived a few minutes later. "You bought a bouquet of purple violets," she said to Ethan, as if the conversation at the traffic light had never been inter-

rupted. "One small bunch of half-wilted purple violets."

Julius noticed then that Lizzie was wearing a
wilted-looking artificial violet in her bright red, curly
hair.

That day they were learning the French words for
the parts of the body. *La tête*. The head. *La main*. The
hand. *Le pied*. The foot.

"Now we will play *un petit jeu*, a little game,"
Madame Cowper announced. "I believe you all know
how to play it. *Allons, debout!* Get up, everybody! You
will form a circle, *un cercle*. And we will play *la version
française* of *le* Hokey Pokey."

The first question that occurred to Julius was: Is this
really happening? Were they really going to put their
right *pied* in, take their right *pied* out, put their right
pied in, and shake it all about?

Apparently they were. Madame Cowper produced a
portable tape player, and pushed the play button, and
the familiar music for the Hokey Pokey began to fill
the room, only whoever was singing it was singing it in
French. Julius tried to listen for words he knew, the
parts-of-the-body words, but they were all jumbled together with the words for *put, in*, and *shake it all
about*. It was easier to watch Madame Cowper and do
what she did.

But Julius almost couldn't bear to watch her shaking

50

different body parts all about. Instead he watched his classmates. Ethan wasn't as good at the Hokey Pokey as he was at frying bacon. He kept getting his body parts in and out a second after everybody else.

Lizzie had managed to find a place next to Ethan in the circle. Julius could tell she was really listening to the tape and trying to hear the announcement of each body part as it came. Her face wore the look of rapt concentration that it did when she was writing her poems.

Alex and Marcia were laughing so hard they could barely turn themselves around for the last line of each verse. The more Madame Cowper shook, the more they laughed. Julius hoped she thought they were laughing at the silliness of the game itself.

The French voice kept on singing. The other kids kept on shaking their body parts. Julius tried to shake the same body parts, but he was one of the world's less talented Hokey Pokey players. If only he could be at the pool doing the backstroke instead.

The tape came to an end. "Monsieur Zimmerman," Madame Cowper said, turning to him.

Uh-oh.

"I think you are having some trouble with *le* Hokey Pokey, *non*?"

Was he supposed to answer? "Um—I guess I got a little mixed up in a couple of places."

"Monsieur Zimmerman, you must listen to the

words—*écoutez bien*—rather than watching your class-mates. *Encore.*"

The music began to play again. Put your something in, put your something out. Julius tried to listen, he really did, but the words ran together so fast he couldn't do it. He stole one glance at Lizzie. She was shaking her foot. He looked again. Her left foot. But now the music was on to the next body part.

Madame Cowper clicked off the tape. She was red and panting from the exertion of Hokey-Pokeying. *"Alors!"* she said. "We have had our exercise for today, *non*? Go outside, *mes enfants*, and have a little recess. If we have time at the end of class, maybe we will do *le* Hokey Pokey again. Monsieur Zimmerman, would you please stay here?"

Alex casually hummed a few bars of Chopin's Funeral March as he headed toward the door with all the others.

When Julius was left alone with Madame Cowper, she said in what was obviously meant to be a kindly tone, *"Maintenant*, Monsieur Zimmerman, we will try it again. *Allons-y!* Come! I will give you *une leçon particulière*, a private lesson, in *le* Hokey Pokey."

Julius knew then that he had reached rock bottom in his life. Lower than a private lesson in *le* Hokey Pokey you could not sink.

The tape began to play. Put your something in.

Julius strained to listen. *Pied? Main? Tête?* Tentatively, he twitched his right foot.

"*Non, non, le pied gauche,* the left foot." Awkwardly, Julius wiggled the other foot. This was like kindergarten, when he couldn't remember which hand he was supposed to put over his heart during the Pledge of Allegiance.

As the tape wore on, Julius shook his way through each body part under the sharp eyes of Madame Cowper, who seemed to be correcting practically every one. By the second time through, he still couldn't hear what that French voice on the tape was saying, but he had managed to get the order of the body parts fairly well memorized. The song ended with shaking your whole self. He knew that much for sure.

As if to celebrate the progress they had made, Madame Cowper joined in on the final verse, shaking her whole self, too. Julius made the mistake of glancing toward the classroom window. Half the class had their faces pressed up against the glass, watching Julius and Madame Cowper shaking themselves frantically in their private little Hokey Pokey duet.

Why couldn't he have learned something useful in French class, such as what the French Foreign Legion was, and how soon he could join it?

6

Edison still howled when his mother left every afternoon and then, three hours later, he howled when
Julius left. This might have shown how attached he
was to his mother and Julius, or it might have shown
how attached he was to howling.

That Monday afternoon, Edison howled as usual
while he watched his mother's station wagon back out
of the driveway. Julius had learned that it was best to
ignore Edison's tantrums. He picked up a few toys
from the family room floor, but Edison, still shrieking,
snatched them out of the toy box and repositioned each
one exactly where it had been before.

Finally, Edison's tantrum subsided. His thumb went into his mouth like a little round plug.

"Hey, buddy," Julius said, "want to go in your stroller to the library?" He needed to get *A Tale of Two Cities* if he was ever going to read it.

"Edison's stroller!" Edison shouted happily. He scrambled up off the floor and ran over cheerfully to stand in front of Julius.

But then his face changed. He pressed his lips together. He shut his eyes. He gave a little grunt. His cheeks turned red.

"No, Edison, no!"

It was too late. An unmistakable odor filled the room. Edison's face looked normal again, or, rather, normal for when he wasn't howling. But Julius could feel all the color draining out of his own. He couldn't believe that little kids could just . . . *go* . . . like that, standing up, in front of other people, their faces giving away the terrible secret of what was going on in their pants.

Julius checked his watch. It was only one-fifteen. Could he really leave Edison like that for two hours and forty-five minutes and then pretend it had just happened? Wouldn't the contents of Edison's diaper be squished in a telltale way by then? Besides, Julius wasn't looking forward to two hours and forty-five minutes spent in the company of someone who smelled the way Edison smelled.

"Edison's stroller!" Edison sang out again, as if nothing had happened. He headed toward the back door, where his stroller stood waiting.

"Wait a minute, buddy! You can't go like that."

Storm clouds gathered over Edison's face. Was it time for tantrum number two already?

"You have . . . you know . . . you can't *sit* in that stuff. I have to—we're going to have to change your diaper."

At least Edison didn't launch into another round of howling. Apparently he didn't mind having his diaper changed. Little kids were strange: they minded stupid, unimportant things, such as having their shirts changed, but they didn't mind catastrophic, cataclysmic disasters, such as having their diapers changed.

Julius followed Edison up to his room. He was going to have to change a diaper. He was just going to have to do it. Every day millions of people in America changed diapers. They survived. Julius would survive, too.

No. He couldn't do it. He wasn't like millions of other people. That millions of people in France spoke French didn't mean Julius could speak French. People were different. Some spoke French, and some didn't. Some changed diapers, and some didn't.

He'd have to call someone to come over and change it for him.

His mother? She had gotten him into this mess in

the first place. And she had to know how to change a diaper, because once upon a time she had changed Julius's own diapers—a sickening thought. So he could call his mother. But, according to his mom, the job was supposed to be teaching him about responsibility. Would she think he was learning about responsibility if he called her for every single catastrophe?

Octavia lived right next door. But she had already said that life was too short for babysitting. And life was definitely too short to deal with the contents of diapers. Maybe Octavia could pretend she was a character in a play and that changing a diaper was part of the script? Julius suspected that there wasn't a single diaper-changing scene anywhere in the complete works of Shakespeare.

His only hope was Ethan. Julius could almost imagine his friend briskly and efficiently changing a diaper, the way he had briskly and efficiently fried the bacon.

Almost, but not quite. But there wasn't anyone else he could call.

"Edison, stay right here. I have to make a phone call. Stay right here and *don't sit down*."

Luckily, Ethan was home and not at the pool.

"What's up?" Ethan asked.

"I'm at Edison Blue's house. There's a problem. A big problem. Can you come over?"

"Sure. What kind of problem?"

Julius had to tell him. Ethan would never forgive him if he didn't. But it was all he could do to say it out loud. "He . . . *went* in his diaper," Julius whispered into the phone. "I have to change it."

There was a long pause on Ethan's end of the line. Then Ethan said, "Number one?"

"Number two." There was another, longer pause. "Listen, if you can't, forget it."

"What's the address?"

Julius told him. Then, weak with gratitude, he hung up.

Upstairs, Julius found Edison sitting on the floor playing with his wooden train tracks. How could he sit in it? And the smell—couldn't he smell himself? Maybe Julius needed to start a list of lifetime goals in the back of his journal.

> *Goals for the Rest of My Life*
> *1. Don't have kids.*

Though maybe he could adopt one who had already been toilet-trained.

A few minutes later, he heard the doorbell. Ethan hadn't wasted any time biking to the rescue. Julius let him in, and the two of them hurried upstairs.

"Edison, this is my friend Ethan. He's going to help me change your diaper."

"No!"

Edison hadn't objected to the prospect of the diaper change before. What was his problem now? Not that Edison was famous for consistency.

"Hi, Edison," Ethan said. "My mom is Mrs. Winfield, your teacher at school."

"My teacher is Patty!" Edison contradicted him.

"That's her! That's my mom!" Ethan said.

"*Not* Mrs. Winfield."

"Patty Winfield. Patty is her first name, Winfield is her last name."

"*Not* Mrs. Winfield!"

Julius decided to cut the conversation short, fascinating as it was. "Okay, buddy, let's get that diaper changed."

"No! *You* don't change Edison's diaper. *Edison* change Edison's diaper!"

Julius thought for a minute. Could Edison really change his own diaper? If he could, Julius's problems were over. Still, he really ought to stick around and supervise, in case anything . . . fell out.

"Okay, Edison, *you* change your diaper. Ethan and I, we're only here to help."

Edison looked suspiciously at Ethan.

"That's right," Ethan confirmed. "We're just your helpers, your diaper-changing helpers."

"Don't look," Edison commanded them.

Julius pretended to shut his eyes, keeping them open just enough to squint through his eyelashes.

Edison pulled down his shorts. Then he tugged at the little sticky tabs on the sides of the diaper.

"Hey," Julius interrupted, "maybe we should do this in the bathroom." Someplace where there wasn't light-colored wall-to-wall carpet.

A brilliant idea he should have had fifteen seconds ago. Off came the diaper, and down onto the middle of the wall-to-wall carpet covering Edison's bedroom floor. Fortunately, it looked as if it fell clean side down.

"Edison need wipes!"

Ethan was able to unroot himself first. He grabbed the box of wipes from the diaper table and placed it on a chair next to Julius.

"Come on, buddy." Julius recovered his voice. "Let's go do this in the bathroom."

"Mommy changes me *here*!"

"Yeah, but Mommy's not changing you now. Julius and Ethan are changing you now—well, helping to change you—and we think we should be doing this in the bathroom."

"No! Here!"

For answer, Julius took Edison by the arm and began to lead him down the hall to the bathroom.

"No!" Edison yanked himself away and tried to run back to his bedroom, his shorts still bunched around his ankles. "Edison do it here! Like Mommy!"

Just as he got back to the bedroom, he tripped and fell, unwiped-bottom side down, and began to howl. But not as loud as Julius and Ethan were howling.

By the end of the afternoon, Julius was pretty certain that there was one thing worse than changing a diaper: scraping and scrubbing the contents of that diaper off a light-colored carpet. He would owe Ethan for this one for the rest of his life.

Luckily, once they managed to open the childproofed cupboard of cleaning products, they found one bottle for removing "pet stains." Apparently, pets stained carpets in much the same way that three-year-olds did. By the time they were done, only a suspicious antiseptic-smelling wet spot on the carpet remained.

When Mrs. Blue came home, Ethan was gone and Edison was getting ready for his closing tantrum. Everything was back to normal. But, not surprisingly, Julius hadn't gotten to the library to check out *A Tale of Two Cities*. He wouldn't have had the strength to start reading it that night, anyway.

7

Julius didn't take Edison to the library until Friday. He would have gone sooner, but the weather turned hot, and he couldn't face the long trudge to the library in the blazing sun when he could lie on the couch in Edison's air-conditioned family room, watching TV. Besides, the diaper episode had definitely unnerved him—not that he had all that much nerve in the first place. What if Edison pooped *again* in his diaper? In public. For example, right in the middle of the children's room at the public library. Julius could imagine the lady from the park appearing out of nowhere to sniff and say, "I think you need to change your little brother."

One thing Julius had to say for that lady, though, was that Edison hadn't thrown any more sand since the incident at the park. They had gone outside to the sandbox twice that week, when Julius had started to feel guilty about all the TV they were watching. Both times Edison had picked up a handful of sand, looked at Julius, then dropped it and looked away. So maybe there was something to the discipline idea, after all. It was worth thinking about.

The heat affected everybody in Intensive Summer Language Learning, too. West Creek Middle School wasn't air-conditioned, so that when it got hot, it got *hot*. Julius felt even sorrier for Madame Cowper when the temperature hit ninety degrees by midmorning. On those days, she didn't just perspire under her arms and on her high, glistening forehead; she sweat all over, so that big, blotchy dark stains appeared on the front and back of the tops of her too-tight polyester pantsuits.

On Friday morning, in French cooking class, the menu was something horrible called a *croque-monsieur*. It was a kind of ham and cheese sandwich on french toast. Julius liked ham and cheese sandwiches and he liked french toast, but he couldn't get used to the idea of the two together. He had to break the eggs for the french toast, and one splattered all over the counter. Still, better one egg on the counter than a whole quiche Lorraine all over the floor.

That day, despite the heat, Julius decided he had better go to the library so he would have something to tell his mother if she asked. He loaded a remarkably cheerful Edison in his stroller, and off they went.

The library was air-conditioned. Every pore of Julius's skin sang with relief as the cool air flowed over him. After the intense midday sun, his eyes took a moment to adjust to the dimmer light inside the library. When they did, he saw Lizzie Archer, curled up on a couch by the window, lost to the world in a book. On the couch facing her, watching him with her dark, amused eyes, sat Octavia Aldridge.

Should he go over and say hi? Julius practiced the line in his head: "Hi." He decided against it. Instead he gave a quick, casual wave and briskly wheeled Edison over to the computer catalog. Luckily, Edison had fallen asleep on the way to the library. With any luck he'd sleep, poop-free, through the whole visit.

Julius typed in DICKENS, CHARLES. The guy had sure written a lot of books. He scrolled down until he found *A Tale of Two Cities*. Status: IN. Julius wasn't surprised. Few people would consider *A Tale of Two Cities* summer reading. He turned from the monitor to find Octavia at his side.

"Hi," he said, glad to have the line ready and rehearsed.

"Hi," she said. *"Comment ça va?"*

Julius didn't miss a beat. *"Très bien, merci, et toi?"*

64

There was a word for how he must look, chatting away in French to Octavia Aldridge, and the word was *debonair*.

Or the word was *idiotic*.

But he did feel a twinge of pride at being able to respond to Octavia so promptly and smoothly in a foreign language. Taking French wouldn't be so bad if he could actually *learn* some.

Octavia peered over his shoulder at the computer monitor. Then she looked at Julius, as if waiting for an explanation.

"My mom thinks I don't read enough."

"Your mom."

Julius remembered that the last time he had talked to Octavia, he had told her that his mom had signed him up to babysit for Edison. He added, defensively, "My friend Ethan said it was pretty good."

"Oh, it's good," Octavia said. "It's great. Almost as great as ice cream. Speaking of which, do you want to go get some? Ice cream. As soon as you get your book."

"Sure," Julius said. Had she just invited him to go out for ice cream? She *had* just invited him to go out for ice cream. "I mean, sure."

Five minutes later, *A Tale of Two Cities* wedged in the stroller next to a still-sleeping Edison, Julius and Octavia entered the ice cream parlor across the street from the library. At that moment an unpleasant thought occurred to Julius. He didn't have any money. His earnings were stashed in a jar in his bureau drawer. All he had with him was fifteen cents.

"What're you going to have?" Octavia asked. "I'm going to have a double scoop of black raspberry."

"Actually . . ." Julius groped again, desperately, in his pocket. All he felt was the same dime and nickel. "I'm not that hungry."

Octavia glared at him. "Then why did you say you'd go for ice cream?"

"Well, I thought I was hungry, but now . . . I'm not."

He searched the menu board for anything that might cost fifteen cents. Then he saw it: water. This was one of the cheapskate places that charged people money for a lousy paper cup of water. "Maybe I'll have some water."

"Water? You're going to watch me eat? And make me feel like a total and complete pig? While you drink water?"

It was time to start over again. "Actually," Julius said, "I *am* hungry."

"A minute ago you actually weren't hungry, and now you actually are hungry?"

"I actually am hungry. But I don't actually have any money. So can I borrow some?"

Octavia laughed. "No. This is my treat."

Even though it charged for water, the ice cream parlor was a pleasant place, with frilly curtains and little old-fashioned wrought-iron tables and chairs. Julius and Octavia claimed a table by the window and pushed the third chair away to make room for Edison's stroller.

Julius took a first lick of black raspberry ice cream. He didn't usually go in for fruity flavors, but he had thought it was safer to order the same thing as Octavia. Of course, once he had ordered it, she had told him, "You don't have to copy me." It was good, though.

"My *Oklahoma!* audition is next week," Octavia said after she had licked her cone down to a manageable point.

Julius thought about mentioning that he was going to be in a play, too, in French, no less. But he could tell it wouldn't impress her.

"What part are you trying out for?" It seemed a good, low-key question to start off with.

"Laurey. That's the lead. Ado Annie is a better part in some ways—you know, she's the one who sings, 'I Cain't Say No'—but there's a long ballet sequence for Laurey, and I can do ballet as well as regular stage dancing."

"Do you think you'll get it?"

Octavia gave him a withering look. "So far in my life, I've been to nine auditions, and I've gotten the part I've tried out for every single time."

"Wow," Julius said, since Octavia obviously expected some response along those lines. But as much as he envied her confidence, it made him a little uneasy, too. What if someday she didn't get a part? He hesitated for a moment, then plunged in. "But nobody gets the part they want *all* the time." Was that true? It sounded true. It sounded almost as true as the law of gravity.

"Maybe nobody *does*. But somebody *could*. Because it all depends on talent, and preparation, and being right for the part. I couldn't get *any* part I tried out for, but if I pick parts that I'm suited for—like Laurey— and prepare like crazy for the audition, which I've been doing, then I'd say my chances are pretty good."

"But what if two people are both suited for a part, and they're both really talented, and they both prepare like crazy?"

"Well, obviously only one of them can get it." Octavia sounded impatient at having to explain such an elementary point to Julius. "All I'm saying is that so far that's never happened to me. I want things more than other people want them, and I'm willing to do what I have to do to get them. Your cone is dripping."

Julius caught the drip with his tongue and for the next minute concentrated on licking his cone. There was no point in trying to challenge Octavia's confidence in herself, and he wasn't even sure why he wanted to. Except it couldn't hurt to consider the idea that sometime in your life something might not work out the way you wanted it to. Julius's own operating principle was that things would never work out the way he wanted them to.

"So why do you like acting so much?" he asked, hoping he was retreating to safer territory. He expected Octavia to toss back some scornful reply, but instead she seemed to be genuinely considering the question.

"Well, partly it's that I like plays so much. I still remember the first one I ever went to. *South Pacific*. I was only four, but one of the teachers in my preschool was in the chorus, so my parents took me, and when the curtain went up . . . it was magic. It was like having a magic ring that could take you to another time and place. And the *music*. Those *songs*. My parents bought me the CD of the first Broadway production, and I learned all the songs by heart, with the same motions I'd seen on the stage. My parents thought it was funny, and they'd put the CD on when their friends came over and have me do my version of 'Some Enchanted Evening' and 'There Is Nothin' Like a Dame.' And their friends would all clap for me, and I'd curtsy, and I knew that this was *it*. This was what I wanted to do with my life."

Octavia stopped. For the first time since Julius had met her, she looked self-conscious. "I bet you didn't expect a speech. Believe it or not, I don't always talk about myself this much. So what about you? Do you have a first memory of something like that?"

Julius tried to think of a memory to match Octavia's. But he knew he had nothing. "Nah," he said.

"What's your very first memory? Any memory. Do you know what it is?"

Julius thought back. His family had moved into their current house when he was three and a half, so any memory of their first house had to be an early one.

"I remember the garage. Our house now has an automatic garage-door opener, but our first house, when I was really little, didn't have one, and I remember my mom getting out of the car and bending down to lift the door and how it came rolling right up."

Octavia stopped licking her cone. "Your first memory is of your garage door?"

Okay, it wasn't much compared with Octavia's memory of *South Pacific*. But she had asked for his first memory, and that was what he had come up with.

Another memory, dimmer than the garage door, began to form.

"Wait a minute. There was a little kid on our street, and there was something wrong with her, or something." It was strange recalling a memory, like watching a picture develop on a Polaroid snapshot. "It was her eyes. They didn't look in the same direction. One of them always turned in. And this other kid—

Jimmy—Jimmy Jardullo—he was laughing at her, and she was crying, so I punched him in the stomach, and I got put in time-out for hitting him, but he didn't get put in time-out for making her cry. I guess my mom thought I felt like punching people in the stomach that day."

Julius stopped. The memory, when it had finally come, had been so vivid, so real. He looked sheepishly at Octavia. "I bet you didn't expect a speech, either."

"I like your memory," she said softly.

"I like yours, too."

Julius heard a howl. Edison was awake, pointing at the remains of Julius's soggy, dripping cone. "Edison wants ice cream!"

"Okay, buddy, calm down, I'll get you some ice cream." He felt in his pockets for his money, then remembered. "Or how about some water? A nice cool cup of yummy water?"

"Edison wants ice cream!"

"Julius." Octavia touched his hand. "I said, this is my treat. What kind of ice cream do you want, Edison? Julius and I had black raspberry."

"*Not* raspberry."

"How about vanilla?" Julius asked.

"*Not* vanilla."

"Listen, buddy," Julius said, "I'll read you the whole list and you pick. Ready? Vanilla."

"*Not* vanilla."

"Chocolate."

"*Not* chocolate."

"Strawberry."

"*Not* strawberry."

Edison had vanilla. It dripped all over him, and all over the stroller, and all over the plastic cover of *A Tale of Two Cities*, but Julius didn't care. He felt too good to care about anything.

"How are you coming along with *A Tale of Two Cities*?" Julius's mother asked him Sunday afternoon, as she was fixing potato salad for a family barbecue that evening.

"Well, I got the book," he said. "From the library," he added, watching the hopeful look fade from her eyes. "I didn't get a chance to go over there until Friday."

"Honey, we *have* the book. It's right there on the bookshelf in the living room."

She put down the mayonnaise spoon and led Julius to the living room, where one whole wall was lined with bookshelves from floor to ceiling.

"Here, with all the other Dickens novels." Sure enough, there was *A Tale of Two Cities*, flanked by *David Copperfield* and *Great Expectations*. "I still remember how long I worked when we moved in to get our books arranged. I had always wanted to live in a house with a library, a real library, the kind with a little moving ladder that rolled from shelf to shelf. I think that's what sold this house to me, all the built-in bookcases."

But there was no moving ladder. Maybe Julius would save his Edison Blue money and buy her one for Christmas. He'd like a moving ladder himself. He would have had a wild time riding on one when he was a little kid.

"Don't you ever browse here?" Julius's mother's tone had shifted from nostalgia to worry. "When I was a child, I read every book my parents owned; I think I read half the books in our tiny public library. And now we have a house full of books, and I sometimes wonder whether you even look at them."

Julius tried to think of something to say to make her feel better. It was true that his mother's books had never had any appeal to him. There were so many of them, all lined up in those long, straight rows, like the army of statues from a dead emperor's tomb he had seen once in the museum. He knew his mother wished he were a reader like—the thought came to him—Lizzie Archer. He could imagine the little squeal of delight Lizzie would give if she ever saw the Zimmermans' books. His mother should have had Lizzie for a daughter. Instead she had Julius for a son.

"I look at them," he said. He looked at the books every day; he just never looked inside them.

As Julius headed upstairs to try to read at least the first chapter of *A Tale of Two Cities* before dinner, he heard his dad say to his mom, "Times have changed, Cindy. A lot of kids today aren't readers."

Julius knew he shouldn't linger at the top of the stairs, but he couldn't help himself. It felt good to hear his dad taking his side.

"There's still nothing like a book," his mom said sorrowfully. "You can't curl up on the couch with a computer. And plenty of kids still read. Ethan read *A Tale of Two Cities* last winter."

Julius should never have told her that.

"It just breaks my heart that Julius doesn't read." Julius could hear the despair in her voice. "When you love something, you can't help but hope your children will love it, too. And children who read do better in school. It's a proven fact. They do."

"But these days, even in schools, kids are watching TV and using the Internet," Julius's dad said gently. "They get their information in other ways."

"Tell me," his mother said, "how much information does someone get from *The Flintstones*?"

"Well, maybe he learns something about the Stone Age."

His dad laughed and, to Julius's relief, his mom laughed, too. Upstairs in his room, he opened his library copy of *A Tale of Two Cities*. "It was the best of times, it was the worst of times." That sounded like a dumb first line to Julius. *Best* and *worst* were opposites. If it was the *best* of times, it couldn't be the *worst* of times. What kind of book began with an outright contradiction?

Julius closed the book. He'd pick it up again later, when his mother's look and tone of disappointment weren't so sharp in his memory.

After dinner, instead of starting in right away on *A Tale of Two Cities*, he made his goals list:

Goals for the Week of June 23–29
1. *Don't go out without money.*
2. *Don't disgrace yourself in French class.*
3. *Don't put off reading* A Tale of Two Cities.
4. *Don't let Edison poop in his diaper again—VERY IMPORTANT!!!!*

Even Julius had to admit that the list was pathetic. Octavia's list—he was sure she had one—would say "Astonish them at the audition for *Oklahoma!*" or

"Memorize all the lines of all the heroines in Shakespeare." Julius's goals were all negative: don't do this, don't do that. It was as bad as the list of rules posted by the side of the pool.

He decided to rewrite the list, making it more positive.

> *Goals for the Week of June 23–29*
> 1. *Carry money with you—at least $2.00.*
> 2. *Do your best in French class.*
> 3. *Read one chapter a day of* A Tale of Two Cities.
> 4. *Toilet-train Edison Blue????!!!!*

The new list looked more impressive. It also looked impossible. Toilet-train Edison Blue? Who was he kidding?

Julius took a five-dollar bill from his Edison Blue jar and stuffed it in the pocket of the jeans he had tossed on the bottom of his bed, the jeans he would wear tomorrow. There. He had already taken care of goal number 1. But goal number 4 was the killer. Goal number 4 was a killer and a half.

When Julius and Ethan arrived at Intensive Summer Language Learning on Monday morning, their classroom had been transformed into an art museum. Every wall was covered with reproductions of what

Julius supposed were great works of French art. He couldn't help but notice that some of the great works of French art featured female persons wearing few, if any, clothes.

"*Ce vendredi*, this Friday, we will go to *le musée d'art*, the museum of art, in Denver, to see an exhibit on *l'impressionnisme français*, French Impressionism," Madame Cowper announced. In her funny mixture of half French, half English, she went on to say that, after touring the exhibit, they would have lunch at a French restaurant; the class would run until three that day. Then Madame Cowper handed out permission slips for the trip, luckily in English.

Julius's first thought was: Edison Blue. Would Mrs. Blue be able to find someone else for that afternoon? Would Edison miss him? Or would he cling as hard to the new babysitter's leg when it was time for him or her to go? Julius was surprised that he almost minded the thought of skipping work. Anyone in his right mind would be overjoyed at the thought of an afternoon without Edison Blue.

Madame Cowper spent the first part of the class talking about French art. One by one, she told the class about each of the pictures displayed in the classroom, even the pictures of the ladies with no clothes on.

"And this is *Odalisque*, by Jean Auguste Dominique Ingres," she said, pointing to a portrait that showed a whole entire naked lady, mostly her back, but one little bit of her front. "Note the exquisite sense of color," Madame Cowper said. Julius chiefly noted the use of a *lot* of skin tones.

"What happened to her clothes?" Alex called out.

To her credit, Madame Cowper didn't blush. "*De l'antiquité*, the human body has always been a favorite subject for *les artistes*."

As Madame Cowper turned to the next picture, Alex shot a rubber band across the room at *Odalisque*. It hit her square on the backside with a loud *ping*.

"Monsieur Ryan! Today I am giving only one warning. If you cannot treat these works of art with the proper respect, you will not accompany us to the museum on Friday." Apparently Madame Cowper could speak in English when she wanted to make a point clear enough. "*Comprenez-vous?* Do you understand?"

Alex glared at her, but she held his gaze. He didn't make any more smart-alecky remarks as she showed the class little naked baby angels on a ceiling painting by Fragonard and naked girls in Tahiti painted by Gauguin. But as the class was getting ready to file outside for the morning break, Alex collected his rubber band from the floor beneath *Odalisque*, and snapped it at one of the naked baby angels.

Instantly Madame Cowper bore down upon him. Julius caught in his breath.

"*Monsieur Ryan, donnez-le-moi.*"

Alex gave her the rubber band.

"*Donnez-moi votre* permission slip."

His face completely sullen and resentful now, Alex returned to his desk, picked up his permission slip, and handed it to Madame Cowper. As the rest of the class stared, she ripped it in half, then in half again, and deposited the pieces in the wastepaper basket.

Alex lost his temper. "You can't stop me from going. This isn't school. My dad *paid* for this class."

"We shall see, Monsieur Ryan, we shall see."

Julius couldn't help but be thankful that for once the person in trouble was not Monsieur Zimmerman. He might not be able to pour quiche or do *le* Hokey Pokey, but at least he was able to stay out of trouble in French class, and to look at French paintings of naked ladies without cracking up.

Julius arrived a few minutes early at Edison's house that afternoon. He wanted a little extra time to talk to Mrs. Blue.

He took a deep breath and made himself start in: "Um—Mrs. Blue—I was wondering—well—do you think it's time for Edison to start using—the—um—the potty?" He kept his voice low so that Edison, busily playing with his trucks at the other end of the room, wouldn't hear.

Mrs. Blue sighed. "I don't know. We bought him a little potty some time ago—you may have seen it in the bathroom—but so far he's shown no interest in using it. And the books I've read all say that parents should wait until the child shows interest. But one of my friends said that her children never showed any interest, so she just had to train them anyway. She used stickers."

"Stickers?"

"As a reward. She made a chart and put it on the refrigerator. But I don't know. Edison is such a sensitive little boy . . . And he gets upset so easily."

Julius wasn't about to disagree.

"Edison's daddy doesn't seem worried about it, but he doesn't really worry about anything. What do *you* think, Julius? You've gotten to know Edison pretty well during the past two weeks. Do *you* think he's ready?"

It took Julius a moment to realize that Edison's mom was actually asking *him*—a twelve-year-old boy— for advice. Somehow he had always assumed that moms just knew these things, like what foods their kids should eat, and what time their kids should go to bed, and when their kids should start using the potty. But Mrs. Blue plainly didn't have a clue.

Julius thought about her question. He was ready for Edison to be potty-trained, but was Edison ready?

"I think so," he finally said. "The other day, when I was changing his diaper, he told me that he wanted to change it himself." Never before had so many grue-some details been left out of a story.

"Maybe you're right. On my way home today, I'll stop and buy some stickers. You might try mentioning it to him—casually at first, so as not to put him off. You know how negative he is."

Julius made no comment.

"Maybe you could play some sitting-on-the-potty games."

"Sure," Julius said, as if he had been playing sitting-on-the-potty games all his life.

Sitting-on-the-potty games sounded pretty terrible, but not as terrible as changing-poopy-diaper games. Julius had taken his first step—a small step, but none-theless a real step—toward his biggest summer goal. It might not be his mother's top-ranked goal for him, but for Julius it would be a real accomplishment.

9

Ever since the conversation in the ice cream parlor, Julius had started actually to like Octavia Aldridge. He had been intrigued by her right from the start: for one, she was beautiful; for another, *she* obviously thought she was terrific. But now he genuinely liked her, too. It seemed impossible that she could ever genuinely like him, and yet she *had* asked him out for ice cream. That, however bizarre and unbelievable, was a fact.

So Julius made a point of suggesting to Edison that they play outside. The heat had broken; the breeze was brisk and refreshing.

"Let's go play outside, buddy."

"No!"

"You can ride your bike." It was just a little plastic trike, and Edison didn't even pedal it; he scooted it along with his feet, like something out of *The Flintstones*. Still, Julius knew that Edison was proud of it.

"No!"

"You can make chalk pictures on the driveway."

"No!"

Desperate, Julius cast about for another idea. "You can . . . sit on your potty."

This suggestion didn't trigger the standard response. "My potty isn't outside."

"We can *take* it outside. Maybe the potty would like to see Edison's yard. Poor potty, stuck all day in a yucky bathroom. Let's take the potty on a little outing."

Edison giggled. Julius took that for a yes.

He got a reasonable amount of sunblock on Edison and then went into the upstairs bathroom to get the potty. It occurred to Julius that emptying that potty would not be appreciably more pleasant than changing a diaper. But he would cross that bridge if he ever came to it.

At the back door, he suddenly had a pang of doubt about carrying the potty into the yard. Forget *A Tale of Two Cities*. He should be reading a book on potty training to see what it said about taking a potty out of the bathroom. You didn't want to make the kid think the whole world was one big bathroom. But you also had to make going to the potty seem like fun.

It was too late, anyway, now that he had said all that stuff about how the potty needed fresh air and sunshine.

"All right, Edison! Out we go!"

In the yard, Edison tried putting the potty in different places: on the patio, next to the grill, in the sandbox, laughing hysterically at each one.

"My potty likes the sandbox," Edison said, still laughing so hard that he almost tumbled over.

"Okay. Leave it in the sandbox. But no throwing sand, potty!"

"Hi, Julius, hi, Edison." Octavia was leaning over the fence. She *would* have to appear in time to overhear Julius engaged in conversation with a potty. Julius was willing to bet things like that had never happened to Romeo. Should he make a joke about it? No. It was better to pretend that the potty wasn't there.

"How's it going?" he asked, getting up and taking a couple of steps away from the potty. That way it wouldn't be in her direct line of vision when she looked at him.

"Fine. Why is there a potty in the middle of the sandbox?"

Edison looked up, evidently pleased at the question. "My potty *likes* the sandbox."

Julius shrugged apologetically, as if he couldn't be expected to understand the strange workings of the three-year-old mind. In a low voice, he said, "We're playing potty games today. You know, to get him used to the idea of using it."

"Potty games." Octavia had a way of repeating Julius's words that made them seem totally inane. Then she laughed, the merry, affectionate laugh he had heard before. "You're a brave man, Julius Zimmerman."

Sheepishly, Julius laughed with her. Her laugh would be a good stage laugh; it made her audience want to join in.

"When is your audition?" Julius asked.

"Wednesday. Down in Denver, at my drama school. My mom works there, so I ride in with her."

"Do they tell you right away if you get it?" He tried to make the question sound casual, but he could tell it annoyed her.

"No, they don't tell you right away if you get it." Her sarcastic mimicry of his words stung. "They'll post the cast list on Friday. Want to hear one of my songs?"

Julius was relieved that her voice had turned friendly again. "Sure."

Lightly, Octavia swung herself over the fence. Julius hoped it was all right. Mrs. Blue had told him he couldn't have friends over during his babysitting hours. Of course, Ethan had come, but that had been a rescue mission, not a social call. And this was a performance, not a social call. And Octavia wasn't exactly a friend. Anyway, it couldn't matter that much which side of the fence she was standing on.

Julius seated himself on Edison's little wooden swing. To his amusement, Edison sat down comfortably on the potty. Julius wondered if Octavia had ever performed to an audience seated on a potty before.

" 'Many a New Day.' " Octavia announced her selection as formally as if they had been in Boettcher Concert Hall in Denver. Then she opened her mouth and sang.

If Julius hadn't decided at the beginning of the summer that he was through with love forever, he would have fallen in love with Octavia the moment the first notes poured out. She had an amazing voice, clear and true and lilting. And her face as she sang was alive with expression, the kind of face a movie camera would love, the kind of face you could watch forever without being bored.

When she finished, Julius applauded, clapping so hard his palms stung. For once agreeable, Edison joined in from his potty-seat perch.

"You'll get the part," Julius said, all doubt banished now. There couldn't be two girls who sang like that and who looked like that when they sang.

"That's the plan," Octavia said. Although she sounded as calm and conceited as ever, it was clear that she was pleased by Julius's response.

"How long does the play run?" he asked.

"Eight performances."

If he weren't through with love, Julius would attend all eight and use his Edison Blue earnings to buy her a bigger bouquet of roses each evening. And on the final night he'd send her so many flowers that her entire dressing room would be filled with them and she'd have to hire a limousine to take them home with her.

It was a good thing that he was through with love.

On Tuesday, apparently daunted by Madame Cowper's swift and terrible punishment of Alex, no one else shot any rubber bands or spitballs at the art pictures.

During the break, Alex announced to the others loudly, "I told my dad that the Cow ripped up my permission slip for Friday, and he's going to call her tonight and make her let me go."

Julius marveled at how differently his own parents would have responded. They would never take his side against a teacher. His mother, especially, always seemed willing to assume that Julius was in the wrong. Julius knew other kids whose parents came complaining to the teacher when they got bad grades. But when Julius got bad grades, his mom came complaining to him.

He was glad they weren't getting a grade in Intensive Summer Language Learning. Though maybe Julius wouldn't have done too badly. He was starting to understand more and more of what Madame Cowper said to the class, and that morning he had had the right answer twice when she called on him.

"Do you think he can?" Ethan asked. "Make her? I mean, it's her class, isn't it?" Julius knew that Ethan's parents were more like his than they were like Alex's.

"My dad's a lawyer," Alex said, "and when he says, 'Jump,' other people say, 'How high?' You'll see. Madame Cowper's going to be the Cow that jumped over the moon."

On Wednesday, Julius realized that he had forgotten to ask Octavia what time her audition was. Morning? Afternoon? He wanted to be able to beam good-luck thoughts to her. Not that she needed luck. As far as Julius was concerned, she was ready for Broadway.

That afternoon, Edison hurried out cheerfully to his potty, still stationed in the sandbox. His new favorite game was to hide things in it. The day before, he had spent the whole afternoon filling the potty with matchbox cars and then taking them out again. He loved best the moment when he raised the lid to reveal his hidden treasures. Today the treasures were pinecones, gathered from under the three tall trees that bordered the Blues' backyard.

Toward three o'clock Octavia appeared in her yard.

"Hey, Octavia!" Julius called over to her, trying not to sound too eager for her news. "How's it going?"

"Okay," she said, coming over to the fence. "Good," she corrected herself. Had Julius imagined a hint of self-doubt in her first reply?

He hoped she would volunteer information about the audition, but when she didn't, he made himself ask, "How was the audition?"

This time she had the correct answer ready: "Fine."

"Fine?"

"It was an audition, all right? I read, I sang, I danced. What else do you want to know?"

"Do you think you did okay?"

"What is this, the Inquisition?"

"It's called friendly interest," Julius said stiffly. Was it too much to assume that he and Octavia were friends?

"Look!" Edison interrupted. As Julius and Octavia watched, he pointed to the potty, filled almost to overflowing with pinecones.

"Wow!" Julius said, as he had the last six times Edison had shown him the pinecones.

"I'm sorry," Octavia said. "All right, since you asked: there was another girl there, who auditioned after me. She was good, that's all."

Julius stopped himself from asking: As good as you

are? And he didn't tell her she was sure to get the part, because he could tell how lame it would sound.

"How're the potty games coming?" Octavia asked then, obviously glad to change the subject.

"Great," Julius said truthfully. Even if Edison never learned to use the potty for its proper purpose, he had been so happily absorbed in playing with it that he hadn't had a single tantrum this week. You couldn't ask much more of a potty than that.

On Thursday Julius was beginning to wonder if the potty that had served as a garage for model cars, a seat in a concert hall, and a storage container for pinecones would ever serve as a potty.

Edison was busy filling the potty with sand, excavated from the sandbox with his toy backhoe. It was hard work for a hot afternoon, and his cheeks were pink with exertion. His hair clung damply to his small head.

"Hey, buddy," Julius began tentatively. "Most people don't put sand in a potty." As if Edison had ever shown any sign of caring about what "most people" did. "You know what most people put in a potty?"

Edison obviously wasn't listening. Julius lowered his voice to a whisper, as if he were about to communicate some fascinating secret. "They put in pee-pee."

At that Edison looked up. "What?"

How much of the speech had Edison missed? Probably the whole thing. But Julius just repeated the last word: "Pee-pee."

Edison burst out laughing, as if *pee-pee* was the funniest word in the English language. Which maybe it was. Then he asked, "What's pee-pee?"

He had to be kidding. Pee-pee was . . . pee-pee. Julius didn't know how to define it for Edison better than that. It was probably one of those words they didn't even put in the dictionary.

"It's a kind of water that you make in your diaper," he finally said.

Suddenly Edison's face cleared. "Wee-wee?" he asked.

"Yes!" Julius should have asked Mrs. Blue what term she used with Edison. "Pee-pee is wee-wee!"

If the word alone had been funny, the sentence defining it was funnier. Edison tried to say it himself, but his tongue tripped over the two rhyming pairs of repeated syllables. "Say it again!" he begged between gasping giggles.

Feeling exceedingly foolish, and hoping that for once Octavia wasn't around to overhear, Julius repeated, "Pee-pee is wee-wee."

"Again! Say it again!"

Okay. Anything in the service of the cause. "Pee-pee is wee-wee."

"Say it again!"

Julius had an inspiration. "Look, I'll say it again *if* you make some pee-pee in your potty." Who needed stickers?

"My potty has sand in it."

"We can take it out. I'll help you."

Eagerly, Julius dumped out the sand. Then, for good measure, he took the potty out of the sandbox and gave it a good dousing with the hose. All clean and empty now, it sparkled invitingly in the afternoon sun.

Not invitingly enough, apparently.

"No!" Edison practically screamed. "Edison doesn't *want* to make pee-pee wee-wee in his potty."

"Okay." Julius tried to keep his voice cheerful. Book or no book, he knew enough about potty-training, or at least potty-training Edison Blue, to realize he shouldn't make an issue of it, lest Edison feel honor-bound to turn against the potty for life. "Whatever you say, buddy. Whenever *you* want to. And when you do, I'll say the funny rhyme again. Deal?"

Edison still glared at him suspiciously, but he didn't howl.

From next door, Julius heard Octavia warbling her warm-up voice exercises, sliding up and down a series of ever-higher scales. If she was still worried about yesterday's audition, it didn't show: her voice rang out loud and clear.

10

Julius's spirits lifted when he saw the school bus parked in front of West Creek Middle School on Friday morning. Yes! They soared still higher when he saw that Alex was not there. Even if the bus was old and bumpy and their destination was just the Denver Art Museum, still, a class trip without Alex Ryan was a clear improvement on ordinary life, at least on ordinary life in Intensive Summer Language Learning.

Mrs. Blue had understood when Julius asked for the afternoon off. She would stay with Edison that day, so Julius didn't have to worry whether Edison would like his new babysitter better, or whether the new babysitter would wonder why there was a sparkling-clean potty in the middle of the sandbox.

Julius and Ethan grabbed two seats together on the bus, as far back as Julius could sit without getting carsick.

"Can you sleep over tomorrow night?" Ethan asked, once Madame Cowper had counted *nez* in French and the bus was on its way.

"Probably," Julius said. "I have to ask my mom. But I think she'll let me. I mean, I have to have *some* fun this summer."

"How's Edison doing?"

"Okay. He's a pretty good kid, really."

Ethan looked skeptical. "Have you had any more . . . problems?"

"Not since the Big One. Right now I'm trying to get him to use the potty."

"Man!"

Julius felt embarrassed by Ethan's admiration, especially since he seemed as far away from that goal as ever. "So Alex isn't here," he said. "I guess his dad didn't call her, after all."

"I bet he did, and she didn't let him push her around. Have you ever met Alex's dad? He's a lot like Alex. The time I saw him, it was at the pool, and he was making fun of Alex in front of all the other guys.

He called him a chicken when he wouldn't jump in the deep end. I'd hate to have a dad like that."

"Me too," Julius said. He thought gratefully of his own gentle, good-natured dad. And even his mother— she was always after him for one thing or another, but she never picked on him in front of anybody else. He had to give her credit for that. He just wished that he could be the son she had always wanted, or else that she could learn to want the son she already had.

"Do your parents bug you about stuff?" Julius asked Ethan.

"Sure," Ethan said. "Not during summer much, but when we're in school, yeah, they bug me about homework, getting it done, checking my work. But not like Alex's dad."

"Sometimes . . ." It was hard for Julius to get the sentence out. "Sometimes I don't think my mom likes me very much."

He thought Ethan might look shocked, but he didn't. All he said was "Oh, moms always love their kids. Just because they yell at us sometimes doesn't mean they don't love us."

Julius knew his mom *loved* him—she still wanted to hug him and kiss him, even though he thought he was too big for that now. But he didn't know if she really *liked* him. His mom liked people who did well in school, people who read books, and not any old books, but long, hard, boring, age-appropriate books.

Julius let the subject drop.

When they got off the bus at the museum, Madame Cowper counted *nez* again. *Vingt-deux*. Twenty-two. Didn't she know that the number would be the same as it had been when they got on the bus, since they had made no stops along the way?

Once inside, Madame Cowper led them grandly to the French Impressionist exhibit, where a museum lady was going to give their group a special tour. The museum lady and Madame Cowper must have been friends, because they acted thrilled when they saw each other.

"Lila!" the museum lady said to Madame Cowper.

"Angie!" Madame Cowper said to the museum lady.

Then they hugged each other. It was embarrassing to watch, but it made Julius feel better to know that Madame Cowper had at least one friend, someone who obviously thought of her as a person, not as a French teacher. Or as a cow. For the first time, he wished Alex were on the trip.

Madame Cowper's friend certainly knew a lot about French Impressionist painting, and Madame Cowper did, too. The pictures themselves were terrific, much better than *Odalisque* or those naked baby angels.

Even when Monet painted the same haystack over and over again, it was always different. The guy could paint. His pictures almost made Julius want to try painting. He could paint a picture of Octavia dancing, like the Degas paintings that hung near the Monets. But painting people had to be harder than painting haystacks. Probably he should start out with haystacks.

The exhibit was a large one, with paintings on loan from museums all over the world. When the tour was over, Madame Cowper counted *nez* again.

"Dix-huit. Dix-neuf. Vingt. Vingt et un."

Twenty-one.

She counted again. *"Vingt et un."* Twenty-one. Who wasn't there?

Ethan was the first to figure out who was missing. "Lizzie," he said.

Madame Cowper gave a cluck of worried irritation. "Monsieur Winfield, Monsieur Zimmerman, would you go back through the galleries to see if perhaps she is lost? The rest of us will wait here."

Together, Ethan and Julius retraced their steps. The galleries had become crowded, and there was no sign of Lizzie anywhere. Then, in the very first gallery, Julius caught a glimpse of her familiar red curls. She was standing, motionless, in front of one of Monet's water lily paintings.

"Hey, Lizzie," Ethan said.

She didn't move.

"Lizzie," he said again, and touched her on the arm.

She gave a little scream. "Ethan?" She looked puzzled to see him.

"Madame Cowper sent us to find you," Ethan said. "The tour is over. We need to get on the bus to go to lunch."

Julius wondered if Lizzie would be upset that she had missed almost the whole tour, and 90 percent of the Impressionist paintings. If she loved paintings so much that she could spend almost two hours in just one room, it was a shame she had missed looking at so many. But she didn't seem to mind. Maybe if you looked at a couple of paintings that long and hard, you didn't need to look at any others.

"I'm never writing poetry again," Lizzie whispered as she followed Ethan and Julius through the museum. Julius glanced at Ethan to see if he looked relieved. Last year, much of Lizzie's poetry had been about Ethan. Ethan mainly looked intent on getting back to the others without losing Lizzie to any more rhapsodies.

"Unless . . ." Lizzie stopped walking, so the boys had to stop, too. "Do you think someone could do *that* with words? Write a poem about water lilies that would make people see them—really *see* them—understand them—the way Monet did?"

Ethan didn't answer, plainly at a loss for what to say.

99

"Maybe," Julius ventured. It seemed a safer answer than yes or no.

Lizzie turned to him. "Do you really think so?"

What Julius really thought was that he hoped the bus hadn't left without them. His stomach yearned for the restaurant.

"Sure," he said.

"Sure," Ethan echoed.

Lizzie sighed blissfully and allowed herself to follow the boys again. If *Ethan* said it, apparently that made it true.

When they rejoined the group, Madame Cowper's face lit up with relief. "Mademoiselle Archer, we were beginning to worry."

"I was looking at the water lilies," Lizzie explained softly.

"Monsieur Zimmerman, Monsieur Winfield, merci beaucoup!" Madame Cowper didn't scold Lizzie for not staying with the group, perhaps because she loved the paintings, too, in her own way, as much as Lizzie did. *"Allons-y!"* she said. *"C'est l'heure du déjeuner.* It is time for our lunch."

Julius couldn't have agreed more.

Julius's family seldom came to Denver, so Julius didn't know the city very well. When the bus stopped to drop them off, he didn't know which part of the city they were in, except that it was some part without skyscrapers or the gold dome of the State Capitol.

After the nose count, the class filed off the bus and waited on the sidewalk for Madame Cowper to lead them to the restaurant. They had walked half a block, past several restaurants and shop windows, when, across the street, Julius saw a girl who from the back looked exactly like Octavia. Could it be Octavia? Her acting school was somewhere in Denver. But what if he called her name and some strange girl turned to look at him scornfully?

What if he called her name and Octavia herself turned to look at him scornfully?

He took the plunge. "Octavia?"

She turned around. It *was* Octavia. And, unbelievably, incomprehensibly, Octavia was crying.

Julius didn't hesitate. He ran up to Ethan. "If Madame Cowper misses me, tell her I'll be there in a few minutes."

"What's happening?"

"I can't talk now. I saw a girl I know, and she's in some kind of trouble."

As Ethan hurried to catch up with the rest of the class, Julius darted across the street to where Octavia was still standing.

Suddenly he knew what was wrong. "You didn't get the part."

101

Octavia turned away from him so he couldn't see her face, but she didn't run away. She just stood there, facing the dingy brick wall of some drab Denver apartment building, sobbing soundlessly.

"Hey," he said gently. What could you say to someone who had had a big disappointment, someone who had never been disappointed before? Every possible line he could think of was inane or insulting. Still, he had to say something. "It'll be okay," he said. Inane *and* insulting.

Octavia whirled around to face him. "No, it won't!" At least she was angry now, rather than defeated.

"All right, it's *not* going to be okay." At that moment, talking to Octavia felt oddly like talking to Edison.

"Oh, shut up." She turned away again, and Julius could tell from her shaking shoulders that she had resumed her silent sobbing.

He tried shutting up, but after a moment of uncomfortable silence, he couldn't help asking, "Did you get *any* part?"

Without turning around, Octavia spat out, "If you can call it a part. Not Laurey, not Annie. I'm in the chorus, but I have a few speaking lines. Do you call that a part? I don't call that a part. I call that a joke."

"Were there some people who didn't get anything?"

The question provoked Octavia to turn around and face Julius again, the better to discharge her fury. "Of *course* there were people who didn't get anything. And

102

I'm supposed to be *happy—grateful—thrilled*—not to be one of them? Lucky me, there are some people in the world who are worse off than I am? Lucky me, at least I'm not starving on the streets of Calcutta?"

The reference to starving made Julius think of the rest of his class, seated in the French restaurant, waiting to order. How angry would Madame Cowper be when this time his turned out to be the missing nose?

But he couldn't leave Octavia in the state she was in. He tried again: "I didn't mean it like that. I meant that I'm your friend"—was that too presumptuous?—"that I *want* to be your friend, and if you feel bad, I feel bad, too. And if I could think of something to say that would make you feel better, I'd say it."

"Oh, Julius." To his shock, Octavia hugged him and then stayed there, within the circle of his arms, leaning against him and crying fresh tears.

"Come on, don't cry." He kept his arms awkwardly in place and struggled to think of something else to say. "Every actress has setbacks, right?" That had to be true.

"I'm not an actress anymore."

"Of course you are."

"No, I'm not." Octavia broke free from Julius. "If I'm going to be a second-rate actress, I'm not going to be an actress at all. Second-rate doesn't happen to be my style."

Were you second-rate because you didn't get one

part? But Julius knew better than to argue with her. He looked down the street, searching for inspiration.

There it was: an ice cream parlor, two doors down. He had already missed the beginning of lunch; he might as well miss the middle of it, too.

"Look," he said, "actress or not, what you need right now is ice cream."

Madame Cowper would be furious with him, even more furious than she had been with Alex. But that couldn't be helped. He'd get Octavia some ice cream, make sure she was okay, and then find the French restaurant—how many French restaurants could there be in that part of Denver?—and try to explain.

11

The restaurant turned out to be easy to find. Luckily, it had a French-restaurant-type name: Chez Jacques. Julius didn't want to go in. Facing Madame Cowper after he had run off on his class trip felt like facing his mother on report card day.

He made himself push open the restaurant door and peer into its dim interior. He could see small tables with red-checked tablecloths; on each one stood a wine bottle holding a candle. Toward the back, a large group was seated at two long tables. His class.

"*Alors!* Monsieur Zimmerman, what have you to say for yourself?" Madame Cowper left the table and came forward magnificently to confront him.

"Nothing," Julius muttered. The less he said, the sooner the conversation would be over with.

"*Rien?* Come, come, Monsieur Zimmerman. We have been waiting for you for *une demi-heure*. Half an hour. You must have some explanation to give us."

When Julius didn't answer, she went on, as if to prompt his memory, "Monsieur Winfield told us that you saw *une amie*. A friend. Is that true, Monsieur Zimmerman?"

Glad that the others were out of hearing, Julius replied, half under his breath, "She was crying, okay?"

"And you leave your class in the middle of a class trip whenever you see *une amie qui pleure*—a friend who cries?"

Well, how often was that? Finding a crying friend on the street in Denver was hardly an everyday occurrence. And finding a crying Octavia was like being struck by lightning and winning the lottery on the same day: the odds were definitely against it.

"Yes," Julius said, a note of defiance in his voice. "I do."

Madame Cowper's expression softened. "*Asseyez-vous, Monsieur Zimmerman*. Sit down. It is too late for you to order a meal—you must tell your friend not to cry so long next time. But perhaps you would care to join us for dessert."

Julius took the seat Ethan had saved for him and

tried, without success, to slip into it inconspicuously as Marcia Faitak giggled and the rest of the class stared. For dessert, everyone ordered crepes filled with various kinds of jam. Julius chose strawberry. It was delicious.

Julius's mother was out at some kind of boring computer meeting all day Friday and Friday evening, too. So Julius didn't see her until Saturday morning, when she settled down on the couch next to him while he was watching some cartoons. He hoped she wouldn't get on his case about watching them. He hadn't seen *Rugrats* in ages.

"So how was the class trip?" she asked him.

"It was okay." He kept one eye on *Rugrats* as he answered. Tommy and Chuckie in their dopey, drooping diapers reminded him now of Edison.

"What was the exhibit like?"

Julius shrugged. "It was a bunch of pictures. Some of them were pretty cool."

"Which was your favorite artist?"

Julius tried to remember the name of the guy who had painted all the haystacks. It started with "M." On the TV, Tommy and Chuckie were stealthily climbing out of their cribs.

"Um . . ." Julius said. "I forget his name."

"Julius!" His mother clicked off the TV with emphatic abruptness. Julius knew she was mad at him now. "What happened to all your goals and resolutions? I thought you were going to give up cartoons this summer. Remember? Less TV, and educational programs only?"

"There's nothing on but cartoons on Saturday mornings," Julius said.

"Then why watch anything?" she said. "Tell me, Julius, tell me honestly, have you read *any* of *A Tale of Two Cities* this summer? Have you read even the first chapter?"

There was no point in stalling. "Well, not yet."

"Three weeks of summer vacation have gone by, and you haven't read anything!"

"I've read a bunch of books to Edison." That much was true. He had started with *Once Upon a Potty*, for obvious reasons, but then he had found a little bookshelf in Edison's room with a whole bunch of books he had loved when he was a little boy: *Mike Mulligan and His Steam Shovel*, *Curious George*, *The Happy Lion*. One afternoon last week he and Edison had been so busy reading the books they had forgotten to watch their cartoons. Did that count?

"Julius, I'm glad you're taking your job seriously, I really am, but when we talked about your reading goals for the summer, we were talking about something more ambitious than picture books."

So it didn't count.

"Julius, I know you have a lot on your plate this summer, and you need some time to relax on the weekends, but it's just as easy to relax with a good book as with TV. Reading is so important! It's the foundation of everything else you do in school, and your schoolwork is the foundation of everything else in your life. Honey, you're going to grow up and have a *job* someday. Have you given any thought to that, any thought at all?"

Julius shook his head. So far all he knew was that he didn't want to write computer manuals like his mom, or be an accountant like his dad.

He hoped his mother wasn't going to cry. That was the worst, when his mother cried. She had cried over his final sixth-grade report card, and the memory of it had made Julius feel sick inside for days. She wasn't crying this time—yet—but she was looking pretty close to it.

As he fiddled with the remote control for the TV, he accidentally turned it on.

"Julius!" His mother snatched the remote away from him and clicked the TV off again. "I think we're going to have to make some *rules* limiting television in this house if your resolutions aren't working. I don't want you watching any more TV until you've made some real progress on your reading goals."

As if to make the banishment of TV more concrete, she laid the remote on the highest shelf of the built-in bookcase in the family room. There might have been something funny about the gesture, for Julius was taller than his mom now and could reach higher than she could. But nothing was funny when his mother was so upset with him.

She stalked out of the room, leaving Julius alone with the blank TV screen.

Should he call Octavia over the weekend to ask her if she was okay? Julius could imagine Octavia giving one of two answers to the question. A scornful no, as in: *Of course I'm not okay. My whole life as an actress has been ruined forever. How could I possibly be okay?* Or a scornful yes, as in: *Oh, that. I've already forgotten about* that. *But thanks for reminding me about one of the most humiliating afternoons of my life.*

He decided against calling.

Midmorning he made himself ask his mother if he could go to Ethan's house. "He asked me yesterday if I could sleep over."

She hesitated.

"I won't watch any TV while I'm there, if you don't want me to."

His mother sighed. "Oh, honey, that's not the issue. Of course you can go, and if Ethan's family is watching TV, you can watch it with them. I really don't want to be an evil ogre here. It's just that cartoons are such a waste of time. They're a complete and utter waste of time. I want you to use your time better than that this summer. And I think turning off the TV here at home is going to help."

She brushed back his hair from his eyes. At least she didn't seem mad anymore.

"You're not mad at me?"

"I'm not mad at you," she said, with an attempt at a smile.

But he knew that even if she wasn't angry at him, she wasn't happy with him, either. By now Julius thought he understood how his mother's mind worked. When she was upset about one thing, it acted as a magnet in her mind for all the other things she had ever been upset about. So he was sure she was walking around thinking: My son likes TV better than reading. My son got three C's on his last report card. My son got nothing at the sixth-grade awards assembly.

Sunday evening, back at home, he remembered to make up his goals list for the coming week. Needless to say, he hadn't made much progress on *A Tale of Two Cities* at Ethan's house, though he had taken the book along with him. Still, carrying it around wasn't the same thing as actually reading it.

Reviewing his other goals: Julius *had* made some progress on toilet-training Edison, though so far nothing had been deposited in the potty besides cars and pinecones and sand. He hadn't humiliated himself a single time in French class, if you didn't count missing half of the class-trip lunch as humiliating. And he had had money with him when he invited Octavia to have ice cream in Denver. The week wasn't a total loss.

Goals for the Week of June 30–July 6
1. *Get Edison to make pee-pee in the potty. Or at least to try.*
2. *Cheer up Octavia. If she still needs cheering up. And if she'll let you be the one to cheer her.*
3. *Keep up the good work in French class (ha ha).*
4. *Read Chapter 1 of* A Tale of Two Cities. *Read it or die!*

On Monday morning Alex was quieter than usual. He must have minded missing the class trip more than he'd let on. He spent the first half of the morning staring down at his desk instead of spouting his usual wisecracks.

At the break, he became more himself again, coming up to Julius to say, "I hear the Cow had a cow on the dumb class trip. Give me five, man." Alex held up his hand; reluctantly, Julius high-fived him. You couldn't leave somebody's hand up there in the air, waiting for nothing.

"It wasn't like that," Julius said then. "I didn't mean to upset anybody. I just saw this friend I had to talk to."

"Yeah, yeah, but first the Lizard gives the Cow the slip, then you."

But Madame Cowper hadn't seemed all that flustered after either incident on the trip. The class trip from hell, Julius knew, would have been one with Alex Ryan on it.

And this morning Madame Cowper seemed positively exuberant. "*Il est temps, mes amis*, it is time, my friends, for us to plan *la présentation spéciale*, the special presentation, which we will give to your families and friends on the last day of class, a week from this Friday."

Was the last day of class coming so soon? Julius had the surprising thought that he would almost miss French class, miss the sight of Madame Cowper adjusting her funny-looking glasses. Since the class trip, when she had been so understanding, Julius had begun to forgive her for the private tutorial in *le* Hokey Pokey.

"So," Madame Cowper went on, "we will sing for your families, yes? And show them our collection of

French paintings? And dance *le* Hokey Pokey. And we will give a performance together of *Cendrillon*."

Julius didn't recognize the name.

"You know it, I believe, as *Cinderella*."

Cinderella! Seventh graders acting out *Cinderella*! The last time they had acted out a fairy tale, Julius remembered, was when they did *Thumbelina* back in second grade. Lizzie was Thumbelina because she was then, as now, the shortest girl in the class.

Apparently oblivious to the horrified silence that had fallen over the room, Madame Cowper began handing out copies of the French script for *Cendrillon*.

"Now, as Cendrillon has *beaucoup de* lines *à dire*, to speak, we must choose a Cendrillon who has shown herself an outstanding pupil of French, *n'est-ce pas*? Is it not so? Mademoiselle Archer, you will be our Cendrillon."

Lizzie flushed with pleasure. At the compliment? Or at the thought of starring in the play?

"Now we must choose our prince," Madame Cowper went on.

Julius shrank back in his seat to make himself as inconspicuous as possible. He knew that every other boy in the class was doing the same.

As Madame Cowper's beady eyes surveyed the room for possible princes, Alex called out nastily, "How about Ethan? He'd make a great prince. He and Lizzie are both short, and besides . . ." He let his voice trail off meaningfully. It was clear that he meant to say they liked each other. Alex had been merciless in teasing Ethan about Lizzie's crush on him last winter.

"Monsieur Winfield," Madame Cowper said approvingly, "will you serve as our prince?"

She didn't wait for an answer. Julius would have defined true misery as the look on Ethan's face when he heard his fate.

Marcia was chosen as the wicked stepmother. Two other girls volunteered to be wicked stepsisters. A pretty girl named Alison was the natural choice as fairy godmother. Julius felt lucky that there were so many more major speaking parts for girls than for boys in *Cinderella*.

"Now we need a rat who will turn into a coachman."

Julius shrank back again, but not far enough, for Madame Cowper said, "Monsieur Zimmerman, will you be our rat?"

At least the rat would have few, if any, lines to speak, unlike the royal trumpeter, who had more lines to speak than any boy except the prince. That part went to a tall kid named Joey. Alex was picked to be one of the mice who became horses. Other boys became pages at the royal court.

As they began laboriously reading through the play,

Julius suddenly thought of Octavia. He and Ethan hated being in plays, but Octavia loved it. Or had loved it. Was she really through with acting? She couldn't be. If only he could find some way to make her see that. The question was: How?

12

By Wednesday, Julius was getting worried. He hadn't caught even a glimpse of Octavia since last Friday's encounter in Denver. He sat on Edison's wooden swing, gazing gloomily at the potty, which that afternoon was filled with erasers. Edison loved erasers, though he didn't use them to erase anything. He just liked clutching them, and lining them up in rows, and, now, putting them in a white plastic potty and then taking them out again.

Julius and Edison were at a stalemate regarding peepee in the potty. So far that week they'd had the same conversation about it every day.

"Say 'Pee-pee is wee-wee,' " Edison would demand.

"I'll say it when you make some pee-pee in the potty," Julius would reply.

"No!" Edison would shout.

And Julius would turn away, trying to act as if he didn't care what Edison decided, either way.

Maybe he *should* call Octavia. Or knock at her door. It would be so easy to walk next door with Edison and ring her doorbell. Edison could even push the button for him. Little kids loved pushing buttons.

No, there was nothing at all hard about it. Except taking the first step. And the next step. And the step after that.

"I have to make wee-wee," Edison announced suddenly. Julius leaped up as if stung by a bee. Edison had never made an announcement about his pee-pee/wee-wee before. He had just *made* it, with no preliminary discussion.

In one swift motion, Julius scooped the erasers out of the potty. "Here?" he asked, his voice practically squeaking from excitement. "Do you want to make it in the potty?"

Maybe he shouldn't ask it as a question. "Here," he said, forcing his voice lower. "You can make it in your potty."

Edison looked at the potty uncertainly.

"Let's take off your diaper," Julius suggested. Edison

could hardly make pee-pee in his potty while he still had his diaper on.

Julius was kneeling down beside Edison to help him undo the sticky flaps on his diaper when Edison said, "I don't have to go anymore."

"Sure you do."

"No I don't."

"You will in another minute."

"No I won't. My wee-wee already came out." Julius groaned. "In my diaper."

More disappointed than he had thought he would be, Julius resumed his seat on the swing. He made a mental note to tell Mrs. Blue to buy Edison those diapers that pulled up and down like underpants. How did any kid in the history of the world ever get toilet-trained when toilet training was so hard?

How did anybody ever do anything when *life* was so hard? Julius's mother was still upset with him. She hadn't made any more critical or nagging comments since Saturday; she hadn't even asked him about *A Tale of Two Cities*, which he still hadn't managed to start reading. But the way she wasn't saying anything gave Julius the distinct impression that his mother had given up on him.

His mother had given up on him, Octavia had given up on acting, Julius was close to giving up on potty-training Edison. The only person who hadn't given up on her projects was Lizzie. During rehearsals, when Cendrillon gazed adoringly at her prince at the ball, it wasn't acting on Lizzie's part, that was for sure.

Lizzie actually made a pretty good Cinderella. She didn't have Octavia's talent for acting, but she was great at memorizing lines. And being picked on by stepmother Marcia and being in love with prince Ethan both came naturally to Lizzie.

The biggest problem with the play right now was Ethan. The problem, to put it bluntly, was that Ethan couldn't act. At all. To save his life. Especially not when he had to act as if he were in love with Lizzie Archer. During rehearsals Ethan forced out his lines as if they were being extracted by torture.

At that moment Julius had the best idea he had had in a long time. What Ethan needed was acting lessons. And the person he needed them from was Octavia.

Was she home? Julius whisked up Edison, whose diaper had the aroma of pee-pee/wee-wee about it, and hurried inside to the phone. From his weekend debates over whether or not to call her, he already knew Octavia's number by heart.

She answered on the second ring. Cowardice overcame Julius. He hung up. But at least he knew she was home.

He called Ethan.

"What's up?" Ethan asked, sounding nervous.

"Nothing," Julius said reassuringly.

"Nothing?" Ethan's voice cracked with relief. "Aren't you at Edison's?"

"Yeah, I'm here. I thought you might want to come over." He'd better not mention the play. "Just to hang out for a while."

"Are you sure it's okay?"

No, he was sure it wasn't okay. Mrs. Blue had told him distinctly that he wasn't supposed to have friends over while he was babysitting. But she hadn't told him he wasn't supposed to go to a friend's house while he was babysitting.

"Actually, we'll come over there."

"Over here? With Edison? You're coming here?"

"Yeah. And . . . I'm bringing another friend, too. See you in ten." And Julius hung up.

Now he had a reason to ring Octavia's doorbell. Or, rather, to let Edison ring it. Five times.

"Oh, it's you," Octavia said ungraciously when she answered it. But Julius almost thought she looked happy to see him. He was certainly happy to see her. She didn't look heartbroken or distraught, or in any way like someone who had shut herself off from the world forever.

"Would you do me a favor?" Julius asked, hoping he would have the nerve to finish the request.

"It depends on what it is."

"You know that French class I'm taking? Well, we're putting on a play, and . . ."

He saw Octavia's face harden. "And?"

Julius made himself continue. "It's *Cinderella*. Only they're calling it *Cendrillon*."

"You're Prince Charming."

He knew he blushed then. "No, I'm the rat who turns into a footman, but my friend Ethan is Prince Charming, only he's not very charming. Partly because in real life Cinderella is in love with him, and in real life he's not in love with Cinderella. Oh, and in real life she's not Cinderella, she's Lizzie. Edison, you can stop ringing the doorbell now."

"And the favor is?"

"I think he needs acting lessons. Edison, that's enough."

"From me."

Julius tried to offer a dazzling smile. "Who better?"

" 'Those who can, do. Those who can't, teach.' Is that the idea? I can't act, so I can teach?"

Leave it to Octavia to twist everything around. "No! That's not the idea. Edison, *stop* it! The idea is—" He broke off. He could hear the incessant ding-dong of the doorbell echoing through Octavia's house. He was certainly glad her parents weren't home.

"The idea is to butter me up and make me believe in myself as an actress again." Octavia's voice was weary now, instead of angry. "Nice try, Julius."

"No! Or, rather, yes, but—anyway, Ethan really does need help. If the prince stinks, the whole play stinks. Couldn't you give him a couple of pointers?"

"When?"

"Now."

Octavia suddenly smiled. "Ice cream afterward?"

Julius felt in his pocket; yes, he had enough money. "Ice cream afterward," he agreed.

Julius pried Edison away from Octavia's doorbell and ignored the howls as he strapped him into the stroller. They were off. Now all Julius had to do was explain to Ethan why he had shown up at his door accompanied by an acting coach who happened to be a gorgeous middle-school girl. But the hardest part was behind him.

They found Ethan shooting baskets in his driveway. Edison's eyes widened when he saw Ethan. "Your mommy is Patty," he said.

Ethan's eyes widened when he saw Octavia. He didn't say anything.

Julius figured he might as well jump in. "This is Octavia. Octavia, Ethan. Octavia is an actress. A really terrific actress. And I thought maybe she could . . ." It was getting hard to finish the sentence. Julius deliberately avoided Ethan's eyes. "Maybe she could give us some help getting ready for the play."

The *us* was a nice touch. Julius didn't need any help

being a rat who turned into a coachman. A rat was just a rat. A coachman was just a coachman. He had only two lines to speak, total.

"Um . . . sure," Ethan said slowly. Julius kept his eyes elsewhere while Ethan led them around to the backyard.

Octavia broke the awkward silence. "Okay. Julius. Let's start with you."

Julius felt alarmed. He had *said* "us," but he hadn't *meant* "us."

"Actually," Julius said, "I only have two lines to speak. The rest of the time I don't say anything."

"That's the hardest kind of acting," Octavia told him. "Mime. All your thoughts and emotions portrayed without words."

"I don't think my characters have any thoughts and emotions."

"Julius. I thought you brought me over to help you. Do you want my help or not?"

He had brought Octavia over to help Ethan—and to help *her*. But if Octavia was bent on helping *him*, he didn't see any way out of it.

"Yes," he said meekly. "I want your help."

He unstrapped Edison from the stroller. Edison immediately began picking the gone-to-seed dandelions next to Ethan's patio and blowing the wispy seeds, with all the breath he could muster, all over the next-door neighbor's immaculate, manicured lawn.

"I'm ready," Julius said.

"You are a rat," Octavia said, fixing her eyes on him. "You have whiskers, and a long tail, and sleek gray fur, and a bad disposition."

Julius stood there, waiting for Octavia to say more.

"Show me," Octavia said. "I see Julius Zimmerman. I want to see a rat. Whiskers, tail, fur, general disagreeableness."

Ethan chuckled. Julius would get him for that later.

"Um—am I . . . should I be on all fours?"

"How many rats do you know who walk on two legs?"

Cursing his long, awkward legs, Julius got down on all fours. He would take the Hokey Pokey over this any day.

"Your tail, Julius. Where's your tail?"

Feebly, Julius twitched his rear end.

"Whiskers."

Feeling the crimson surge into his face, Julius made an attempt at twitching his nose.

"That's better. Good! Now look furtive."

Julius wasn't sure what the word meant.

"Sly. Sneaky. Used to darting behind the woodwork. Knowing that Cinderella's stepmother will throw a shoe at you if she sees you. Looking for treasures to steal. Willing to bite if cornered."

Julius tried to put an expression on his red, twitching face that would convey all those things. He didn't need Octavia to tell him that he failed miserably. He didn't need Ethan to tell him that he looked ridiculous.

"I'll show you." Octavia flung herself down on all fours. Before Julius's eyes, she became a rat. How she did it, Julius didn't know, but he saw her long, thin tail and quivering whiskers and beady eyes. As Julius and Ethan stared, Octavia constructed an elaborate pantomime, sniffing about for food, darting behind one of Ethan's bushes at an imagined sound, greedily snatching up a stray morsel of cheese and devouring it with her sharp rodent's teeth.

Then, as suddenly as she had become a rat, she was a girl again.

"Like that," Octavia told Julius.

Oh. Like that.

Julius tried once more, but it was Edison who really seemed to have taken Octavia's demonstration to heart. Down on his hands and knees, with his diapered bottom twitching in the air, he looked more like a little rat than Julius ever could.

But Octavia was full of encouragement. "That's it, Julius! Yes, Edison! Twitch those tails!"

Then Octavia turned to Ethan. By the time she was done with him, he sounded considerably more like a lovesick prince than he had before. However, the real test would come when he had to say his lines not to Octavia but to Lizzie Archer. It was easy, Julius thought, to act as if you were in love with Octavia. He felt almost jealous watching Octavia and Ethan rehearsing their scenes together.

Ethan didn't join them for ice cream, though he flashed Julius a quick thumb's-up sign of approval when Octavia's back was turned. For once, Julius was eager to leave his friend behind.

Octavia showed her merry side at the ice cream parlor. She kept Edison amused the whole time by speaking in different accents, from a Southern drawl to upper-class English to the talk of a tough New Yorker.

But then Julius made his big mistake. "You're a great actress, Octavia. You know you are. Just because you didn't get one part in one play—"

Octavia cut him off. "Give up, Julius. I'm not a great actress, not that *you* would know a great actress if you saw one."

Julius knew Octavia was so cutting because his clumsy words had opened her wound. He'd thought maybe she had healed by now. Apparently she hadn't.

13

When Julius made his goals for the week of July 7–13, he had an easy time doing it. The only thing he wrote in his journal was:

> *Goals for the Week of July 7–13*
> *See Goals for the Week of June 30– July 6.*

Edison still hadn't made pee-pee in the potty. Octavia still wasn't cheered up. Maybe getting Octavia to help Ethan with the play counted as keeping up the good work in French class; in any case, Julius needed to keep it up some more. And he still hadn't started *A*

Tale of Two Cities. He just couldn't make himself do it. Every time he opened the book, he felt overcome by the weight of his mother's disappointment in him. The book lay on his bedside table, like a silent reproach, saying to him all the things his mother wasn't letting herself say.

He picked up his pen and added a fifth goal:

5. Help my mom feel better about

About what? About having a son who was a mediocre student at best and who didn't like to read and who got a two-line part in the *Cendrillon* play because his French accent was so bad? But he couldn't write all of that in his goals list. So he wrote:

5. Help my mom feel better about things.

On Monday, after another afternoon in which Edison's pee-pee came out in his diaper, but not in his potty, Julius was almost ready to give up on goal number 1.

Mrs. Blue seemed ready to give up, as well. As soon as she returned home and gave Edison his hug and kiss, she turned to Julius. "Any luck?"

He knew what the question meant. "No," he told her.

Mrs. Blue put Edison down. He ran back to his potty, which now stood in the middle of the family room, still filled with erasers.

"Oh, Julius, I had such a feeling that it would happen today, while you were here. You know, another boy, an older boy, someone he looks up to."

"It'll happen," Julius said, sounding more confident than he felt. "He won't be going off to college wearing diapers." He had heard this kind of remark made to other mothers about other things. He even remembered neighbor ladies telling his own mother, when she had worried about his thumb-sucking, "Well, he won't be going off to college sucking his thumb."

"It's not college I'm worried about, it's kindergarten," Mrs. Blue said miserably.

"That's still two years away. A lot can happen in two years."

"Oh, Julius." Mrs. Blue seemed close to tears. What was it about Julius that attracted crying females? "It's so hard being a mother sometimes. I lie awake at night, wondering if Edison will ever use the potty, if he'll ever stop being so negative, if he'll ever outgrow biting."

"He doesn't bite me anymore," Julius offered. "He hasn't done it since the first week." If it was hard to be a mother generally, how much harder it must be to be the mother of Edison Blue.

Or of Julius Zimmerman?

"Sometimes I think that if he would just make wee-

wee in the potty, I'd never worry about anything else ever again." She laughed. "Famous last words."

"It'll happen." Julius hoped it would happen before Edison went off to kindergarten. What he really hoped was that it would happen that summer. While he was babysitting. So that there would be one shining moment of achievement in his sixth-grade summer.

"Listen," Julius said awkwardly. "This French class I'm taking? We're putting on this play on Friday, you know, to show our families and friends what we've learned about French language and culture. We're doing *Cinderella*, in French, and I only speak two lines, but I'm the rat who turns into a coachman, and, anyway, if you think Edison might like it . . ."

"He'd love it!" Mrs. Blue said. "I can take off work that morning. Edison, honey, Julius is going to be in a play! He's going to be the rat in *Cinderella*! Do you want to go see him? Mommy will take you on Friday."

"No," Edison said.

"You don't want to see Julius being a rat?"

"Yes," Edison said then.

"Yes, you don't want to see the play, or yes, you do want to see the play?" Julius asked him.

"I want to see it," Edison said.

On Tuesday, Julius debated with himself for the better part of the afternoon whether or not to leave an invitation to the play in Octavia's mailbox. While Edison loaded up his potty with small plastic action figures, Julius took one of the flyers Madame Cowper had given the class and tentatively wrote Octavia's name on the back of it. Then, at the bottom, hoping it didn't sound too mushy, he wrote:

> *Thanks for all your help. Ethan is a great prince now. I am getting better with my tail, too.*

He hesitated, then added:

> *You are a wonderful actress, whatever you say.*
> *Sincerely,*
> *Julius Zimmerman*

Not that saying it would make her believe it. He could hear her mocking voice in reply: "Thank you, Julius. If *you* believe in me, then of course I should believe in myself."

Before he could change his mind, he scooped up Edison, went next door, and slipped the flyer in Octavia's mail slot, careful not to let Edison ring her doorbell even a single time.

Instantly he was sorry he had done it. But the worst thing that could happen was that she would tear up the invitation and not come to the play. She probably couldn't come, anyway.

. . .

Ethan was a good prince now, if not a great one. Julius was an adequate rat now, if not a good one. Lizzie's French lines tripped off her tongue as fluidly as if she had been born in Paris, helped no doubt by all the time she had spent selling flowers there in her dreams.

One thing still bothered Julius. At every class concert or play that he had ever seen, somebody came up to the microphone and made a speech thanking the teacher and giving her a present from the class. Somebody's mother always made sure it happened. This time nobody seemed to be making sure it happened. Julius hoped it wasn't up to him to do it. Or was that what his mother meant by learning about responsibility?

During the break on Tuesday, Julius tried broaching the subject with some of the others.

"Do you think . . ." Julius began, wishing that he had the kind of voice that would make people take seriously any idea that came from his lips. He didn't. "Do you think we should get a present for Madame Cowper, you know, to give her at the play?"

Ethan said right away, "Yeah. Like all chip in a dollar for it."

Quickly Julius called the rest of the class over to join them. "Hey, guys? Do you want to chip in a dollar to buy Madame Cowper a thank-you present?"

"You're kidding, aren't you?" Alex asked. "Tell me you're kidding."

"No," Julius said. "I'm not kidding. Look, you don't have to contribute if you don't want to."

Lizzie was the first to produce her dollar. Some kids told Julius they needed to get their money from home, but promised to bring it tomorrow. Alex ended up being the only kid to refuse. Fine! Julius figured they could get a pretty terrific present for twenty-two dollars, a dollar for every *nez* in the class except one.

That evening, after supper, Julius went up to his room and took *A Tale of Two Cities* off his bedside table. *Read it or die!*

He was pleasantly surprised to discover, when he actually made himself open the book, that the whole first chapter had only three pages. If he had known that, he would have forced himself through it weeks ago. He forced himself through it now, and found that not only was it much shorter than he had feared, it was also much more boring—something about a Woodman and a Farmer, and the year of Our Lord one thousand seven hundred and seventy-five. Why not just say "1775"? What was the point of writing in such a long-winded way?

Julius pushed on to Chapter 2. It was a little bit better, because at least there was some dialogue in it, between some people named Tom and Joe and Jerry. But he didn't get the sense that they were main characters, and he still didn't have the faintest idea what was supposed to be happening. Had Ethan really read this book and *liked* it? It was hard to believe.

At the end of Chapter 3, Julius gave up. What was the point? There were forty-five chapters in all, which meant that, with three down, there were still forty-two to go. Forty-two! Grimly, he opened his goals journal and crossed off goal number 4. But he felt no surge of satisfaction. A great classic of world literature, one of his mother's all-time favorite books, and it was all he could do to get through three chapters of it.

On Wednesday Edison announced three different times that he needed to use the potty. Three different times Julius rushed to help Edison whip off his pull-on diaper and ready himself for the Big Moment. Three different times the Big Moment didn't come.

Edison looked as downcast as Julius felt. "My wee-wee doesn't like potties," he said sorrowfully. "My wee-wee just likes diapers."

"It has to learn to like potties," Julius said. "That's all. It takes time for it to learn. Give it time."

But not too much time. Julius couldn't take any more of watching Mrs. Blue's face fall when she came home to discover, once again, that Edison's diaper was wet and Edison's potty was dry.

"Oh, Julius," she said to him later that afternoon as he was getting ready to go home, "Jackie across the street told me that her little girl trained herself—trained herself completely—when she had just turned two."

"Well, girls are different." It was another line he remembered people telling his mother, when he'd had trouble learning to write in cursive back in third grade. They would tell her boys had more trouble learning cursive than girls did—conveniently ignoring that all the other boys in Julius's class could write in cursive.

"I guess so," Mrs. Blue said. "I asked Patty Winfield at Little Wonders, and she said this was normal, that some children don't learn till they're four. Four!"

Julius tried to put on a sympathetic face, but four didn't sound so old to him. Four was nothing. Four was a million years ago, when life was simple and no one expected you to teach little kids to use the potty or to talk in French or to read four-hundred-page-long novels by Charles Dickens.

"Dad and I are both planning on coming to your program this Friday," Julius's mother told him that night at dinner.

"You don't have to do that," Julius said. "I only have two lines to speak in the play. 'Cinderella, your coach is here.' And 'Off to the ball!' You don't have to miss work to hear me speak two lines."

"But there's more to the program than the play, isn't there?" his mother asked.

"We sing some songs, and we . . ." He could hardly bring himself to say it. "We do the Hokey Pokey in French."

A smothered guffaw came from his dad.

"So it's really okay if you don't come," Julius concluded.

"I don't often get the chance to see the Hokey Pokey done in French," his dad said. "I'll be there."

"Do you realize," his mother asked, "that when your class ends on Friday, summer vacation will be half over?" She hesitated. "Are you making any progress on your summer goals? Now that we've turned off the TV, you haven't had as many distractions."

Julius thought about the dry potty, about Octavia's depression, about *A Tale of Two Cities*, which he knew now he would never finish.

"Not really," he admitted. "I mean, I've been making lists every week in my journal, but . . ." He trailed off.

"This is your big chance, Julius," his mother said, a note of desperation creeping into her voice. "A whole summer to work on those academic skills you're going to need for seventh grade, to get ready to make a new start in school next year." As if afraid she would say more, she got up to start clearing the table.

"Look, honey, he's taking a class, working a job ... And he's only twelve," his dad said gently.

"Twelve!" his mother said. She sounded like Mrs. Blue saying, "Four!" "When I was twelve ..." This time she was the one who trailed off.

"When you were twelve, you were perfect." Julius finished the sentence for her, surprised at the intensity of his own response. "When you were twelve, you read books all day long, and you won prizes, and your mother bragged to all her friends about how wonderful you were."

He tried to stop himself, but the words, held in too long, came tumbling out: "Well, you want to know something? I'm not you."

"Julius." His mother reached out her hand to him, but he didn't take it. Instead he left the table and went upstairs to his room, trying not to indulge in the childish satisfaction of slamming the door.

There, he opened his goals journal and ripped out the five pages he had written so far that summer. He crumpled them into five little balls and hurled them, one by one, at his wastepaper basket.

For the first time in his life, his aim was perfect.

Ten minutes later, he heard his mother's soft knock at his door. He wanted to tell her to go away. Instead he mumbled, "Come in."

"May I sit down?" she asked him. Her eyes were red and glistening, as if she had been crying. For answer, Julius sat up on his bed and moved over to make room for her.

"Julius."

He stared down at his bare feet.

"Julius, I'm sorry if I've put too much pressure on you this summer. God knows, I've made mistakes over the years. But I'm your mother. It's my job to try to help you grow and develop into all you can be."

"I know," Julius said. He hoped she wouldn't start in on the speech about reading.

Sure enough, she did. "It's just that reading—well, reading is so important, Julius, for whatever else you decide to do in your life. And reading is—if you love to read, then the whole world is open to you. It's all there, everything is there, in books. I know you haven't had a lot of time to read this summer. Maybe I shouldn't have signed you up for a class *and* a job. Anyway, whatever I did, I did because I thought it was best for you."

"I know," Julius said again. She didn't understand that it wasn't the class or the job that he minded; it was thinking that whatever he did, it wasn't enough to please her, could never be enough, because he wasn't the person she wanted him to be.

"I won't ask you about your reading again," his

mother said. She gave a wry, wan smile. "Or at least I'll try hard not to. Okay?"

"Okay," Julius said. He made himself return her smile, over the lump in his throat.

After she left, he stared down again at his feet. He knew she was trying to be a good mother to him, the way Mrs. Blue was trying to be a good mother to Edison. He just wished she could see that, in his own way, he was trying, too.

14

On Friday morning Julius was more nervous than he had thought he'd be.

What if Octavia came? What if Octavia didn't come?

Would Madame Cowper like her present? Julius had thought it was perfect when he found it at the mall yesterday afternoon, but what did he know about anything? And would he make a fool of himself giving it to her?

Would Madame Cowper tell his parents that he had run off with Octavia on the class trip? That would hardly be a story to gladden his mother's heart. Would his mother be disappointed in him yet again when she heard him stammer his two pathetic lines in the play, with the worst French accent in the class?

When Ethan came to get Julius so they could ride to school together, Ethan looked as miserable as Julius felt. His face bore the set look of a soldier about to have his leg amputated without anesthesia.

"It'll be over in three hours," Julius told him, trying to sound encouraging.

"One hundred and eighty minutes," Ethan said. "Ten thousand eight hundred seconds."

Put that way, it didn't sound encouraging at all.

In the classroom, all was chaos, as kids muttered their lines to themselves and scrambled into their makeshift costumes. Julius wore black sweatpants and a black sweatshirt to be the rat, with a rat mask he had made out of a paper bag. Once he became the coachman, he would quickly slip off his mask and slip on a fancy jacket that Madame Cowper said belonged to her husband. So there was a Monsieur Cowper. That was a strange thought.

Ethan wore a prince costume loaned by the middle-school drama teacher, with the pants pinned up because Ethan was shorter than the typical middle-school prince. Lizzie had brought in her own rags —maybe the ones she had worn in her garret in Paris?—but her ball gown was also a drama department loan. She actually looked pretty when she had it on, with her blue eyes blazingly bright and her red curls bouncing. Julius wondered if Ethan had noticed.

The program would be performed in the school all-purpose room. The first guests began arriving at ten. Julius waved to his parents, glad that Madame Cowper was too busy with last-minute costume adjustments to chat with anybody. So far, so good. He saw Ethan's mom and older brother, Peter; Ethan's dad had to work. He recognized Lizzie's mother, short, like Lizzie, with hair almost as red.

"Julius! Julius! Julius!"

Edison ran up to him, and, touched by the exuberance of the greeting, Julius swung him up for a hug. Behind Edison came Mrs. Blue, looking sheepish, pulling Edison's little red wagon.

In the little red wagon sat Edison's potty.

"One of my parenting magazines came yesterday," Mrs. Blue began apologetically, "and it had an article on toilet training, and it said that for the crucial first weeks of training, it's important not to go away from home, and if you do go, to take the potty with you."

Julius stared at her.

"I hope you don't mind," Mrs. Blue said, her face suddenly anxious.

"Mind? No! Of course not!" If Alex found out that one of Julius's guests for the play was a potty, and teased him about it for the rest of his life, that was the way it would be.

"My potty likes plays!" Edison said. Julius had never

realized how piercing Edison's high little voice was until he uttered this particular sentence in hearing range of all Julius's classmates.

"Well, I hope it will like this one," Julius told him.

Back with his class again, he scanned the room for Octavia. Remarks about potties were usually her cue for a grand entrance. He didn't see her anywhere.

Not that he had thought she would come.

Only he *had* thought she would come.

In any case, she wasn't there.

It was time for the program to begin. Madame Cowper, magnificent in a flowing Moroccan caftan, which suited her better than her usual pantsuits, stepped up to the microphone. She beckoned to the cast, in their costumes, to crowd around her.

"*Bonjour, mesdames et messieurs, amis et familles*, friends and families. Today we present for you *une petite pièce*, a little play." She went on with a speech about all they had learned in the past five weeks and about how much she had enjoyed having them as students. Julius knew she couldn't have enjoyed having him as a student—someone who couldn't put a quiche in the oven without spilling it all over the floor, someone who couldn't even put his right foot in and take his right foot out.

As Madame Cowper's speech wound to a close, Julius's palms turned clammy. It was time for him to make his speech. Since it was his idea to give Madame Cowper the present, he felt it was his responsibility to do it.

"*Excusez-moi,*" Julius said, stepping forward from the rest. "*Nous avons un cadeau pour vous.* We have a present for you. *Merci beaucoup.* Thank you very much." He felt foolish saying it in French, especially in *his* French, but he had decided to do the thing all the way if he was going to do it at all.

"*Un cadeau? Pour moi?*"

Madame Cowper sounded so genuinely pleased and surprised that Julius wondered fleetingly what Alex was thinking right then. Was he a little bit sorry he hadn't contributed anything?

She tore off the wrapping paper and lifted the top of the box. Then she pulled out a scarf with Monet's water lilies printed on it. Julius hadn't been able to believe his eyes when he had found it on sale in the regular department store in the mall.

"Ohhh!" Madame Cowper gave a long sigh of ecstatic appreciation, sounding almost like Lizzie Archer, as she held up the scarf for everyone to see. The applause was loud and long. Ethan and Lizzie were clapping hardest, of course, but the others were clapping as well, including Marcia. Even Alex was clapping, as hard as if he had picked out the present himself and helped to pay for it.

The play began. Lizzie-as-Cinderella sat alone in her ashes. Marcia-as-wicked-stepmother was mean to her. So far it seemed like ordinary school. During his few moments onstage, Julius acted as much as he could like a rat, even though Octavia wasn't there to critique his tail. Cinderella's fairy godmother appeared. Yes, Cinderella *was* going to the ball!

Just as Julius whipped off his rat mask and got ready to whip on his coachman jacket, a piercing little voice from the side of the stage summoned him.

"Julius, my wee-wee is ready to come out!"

Mrs. Blue had hurried after Edison and was trying to shush him. "Edison, Julius has to be in the play now, honey!"

Edison, hopping from one foot to another, clutching his shorts, looked exceedingly like a toddler who had to go.

"I want my wee-wee to come out in my potty!" Edison wailed.

Julius shot a frantic look at the fairy godmother. She was still working on transforming Cinderella's rags into a ball gown. He had a minute, maybe two.

He dropped his jacket and mask, slipped off the stage, and raced with Edison, Mrs. Blue, and the little red wagon out to the hall.

"Oh, Julius—do you think . . . ?" Mrs. Blue breathed.

Julius expertly tugged at Edison's pull-on diaper and positioned the potty for him to sit on.

There came a small tinkling sound that could mean only one thing.

"It came out!" Edison danced around his potty as best he could with his shorts and diaper still bunched around his ankles. "Look, Julius, look! My wee-wee came out!"

Julius looked, hoping this was the last time in his life he would be called upon to admire anyone's wee-wee. Then, from inside the all-purpose room, he heard the fairy godmother's voice, tinged with exasperation, announcing in emphatic French that *now* this rat would become a coachman.

Oops!

Julius sprinted back to the stage. Panting, he shrugged into his jacket and presented himself to the irate fairy godmother.

A long silence followed. Wasn't somebody supposed to say something?

He was supposed to say something. Lizzie, radiant in her ball gown, whispered the line to him: *"Cendrillon, votre carrosse est ici!"* Julius gasped it out.

He was supposed to say another line, too. Now, or later on?

There was another long silence.

Okay, he was supposed to say it now.

"Allons au bal!" Julius said.

At last the play was over, and all that was left was *le* Hokey Pokey. Julius shook his body parts as best he could, knowing that half the time he was putting the right foot in when he was supposed to be taking the left foot out. The reality of what had happened outside in the hall finally hit him. Edison had made pee-pee in the potty! And the glory of that moment belonged to him, Julius!

When they returned for refreshments back in their classroom, Julius grabbed a croissant. He took one big buttery bite and turned around to find his mother standing right in front of him.

"Oh, Julius," she said. Her "Oh, Julius" carried such a different meaning from Mrs. Blue's "Oh, Julius."

"Where did you go? I felt so sorry for that girl playing the fairy godmother. She stood there without the faintest idea what to do."

His mother looked as if she was trying to keep herself from saying more, but she couldn't do it. "Julius, the whole point of the babysitting job was to help you learn to be more responsible. Oh, Julius, what am I going to do with you?"

"Nothing, I guess," Julius muttered. "There's nothing you can do with me." His post–pee-pee exhilaration had evaporated.

He felt someone tugging at his leg. Edison. The little boy's tight hug brought to Julius's eyes the tears that hadn't come with his mother's scolding.

Mrs. Blue put her hand on Julius's mother's arm. "You must be very proud of Julius."

Julius's mother hesitated before responding, as if wondering what feature of Julius's performance in the play or the Hokey Pokey could have inspired such a comment. "Oh, we are," she said slowly.

"He is just working wonders with Edison this summer. Edison is blossoming because of Julius. That's the only word for it. Blossoming. And do you know what happened just now?" Mrs. Blue lowered her voice as if the miracle about to be revealed were too sacred to be spoken out loud.

"Edison used the potty! For the first time! Right now! During the play! And Julius was kind enough to rush away from the play to help him do it. I don't know any other boy his age who could give so much to a young child. Julius, I can't thank you enough for this morning, and for everything."

Julius let himself look at his mother. Now *she* looked ready to cry.

"I think Julius has a gift, a real gift, for working with children," Mrs. Blue went on. "I was telling Patty Winfield about him, and she said Edison talks about Julius all the time at school, too. Patty said when Julius is old enough to get a real summer job, she'd be glad to help him get one at Little Wonders."

A job working with lots of little kids like Edison Blue, all day long? Julius never would have believed that the thought of it could make a slow smile spread across his face.

His dad came up to them then. "Son, I sure enjoyed that Hokey Pokey," he said with a big grin.

As Julius's dad led Mrs. Blue and Edison to the refreshment table, Madame Cowper appeared and pumped Julius's mother's hand. For a moment, Julius thought she was going to kiss his mother on both cheeks, but she didn't. "Madame Zimmerman, I have so enjoyed knowing Julius."

Was she kidding?

Madame Cowper put her arm around Julius's shoulder. *"Julius a un grand coeur."* She said the words with unusual distinctness, to help Julius's mother understand what she was saying. She couldn't, of course. Julius couldn't, either.

"Julius has a big heart," she translated, with the same exaggerated emphasis on each word. "On our class trip, he leaves us. For half an hour, he leaves us. I worry, I fret, my hair turns gray. Why does he leave us? Because he sees a friend, and she is crying. That is Julius."

Madame Cowper fingered the Monet scarf, which she had tied around her neck. "And this scarf. It is not an easy task to find the right present for *une femme d'un certain âge.* An old woman. A woman whom some call the Cow. Eh? *Non,* Julius Zimmerman, he has a big heart."

With that, she left to talk to other parents.

"Oh, Julius."

He turned to face his mother.

"I had no idea . . . Somehow I thought . . . I thought things this summer *weren't* working out for you. Did you really toilet-train Edison? And all those things your teacher said . . . Oh, Julius, you and I are so different, it's hard for me sometimes to see that—well, your goals may not be the goals I picked for you, but they're *your* goals, and I'm proud of you for accomplishing them. I hope you know that. I'm proud of *you*."

She reached out her arms to him, and Julius gave her a quick, stiff hug, then pulled away, to bring himself back under control.

It wasn't turning out to be such a bad summer. Intensive Summer Language Learning and Edison Blue had both been his mother's ideas, but Julius had to admit they had worked out all right in the end, even if they hadn't worked out exactly the way his mother had planned. Unbelievable as it seemed, he had accomplished almost everything on his goals list. He had redeemed himself in French class and even learned some French. Edison had used the potty. His mother understood him a little better.

The only things he hadn't done were cheer up Octavia and read *A Tale of Two Cities*. He'd return the book tomorrow; maybe he'd check out some books on child development instead.

Mrs. Blue returned and touched his elbow. "I almost forgot to give you this."

It was a folded piece of paper. Julius opened it and read:

> *Dear Julius,*
>
> *I'm so sorry I can't be at your play today.*
> *Twitch that tail for me!*
> *The reason I can't be there is because I have an audition in Denver. Wish me luck!*
>
> *Octavia*
>
> *P.S. If I get the part, I'll buy you ice cream.*
> *P.P.S. If I don't get the part, I'll buy you ice cream.*

Edison tugged at Julius's leg again, and Julius picked him up for another hug.